Tin-Types Taken

Streets of New York

A Series of Stories and Sketches Portraying

Many Singular Phases of Metropolitan Life

Lemuel Ely Quigg

Alpha Editions

This edition published in 2023

ISBN : 9789362090522

Design and Setting By
Alpha Editions
www.alphaedis.com
Email - info@alphaedis.com

I.

MR. RICKETTY.

Mr. Ricketty is composed of angles. From his high silk hat worn into dulness, through his black frock coat worn into brightness, along each leg of his broad-checked trowsers worn into rustiness, down into his flat, multi-patched boots, he is a long series of unrelieved angles.

Tipped on the back of his head, but well down over it, he wears an antique high hat, which has assumed that patient, resigned expression occasionally to be observed in the face of some venerable mule, which, having long and hopelessly struggled to free herself of a despicable bondage, at last bows submissively to the inevitable and trudges bravely on till she dies in her tracks.

Everything about Mr. Ricketty, indeed, appears to have an individual expression. His heavily lined, indented brow comes out in a sharp angle over his snappy black eyes, which, sunk far within their sockets, look just like black beans in an elsewise empty eggshell.

His nose is sharp, thin, pendent, and exceedingly ample in its proportions, and it comes inquiringly out from his face as if employed by the rest of his features as a sort of picket sentinel.

It is that uncommonly knowing nose to which the prudent observer of Mr. Ricketty would give his closest attention. He would look at the acute interior angle which it formed at the eyes, and think it much too acute to be pleasant and much too interior to be pretty. He would look at the obtuse exterior angle which it formed on its bridge, and wonder how any humane parent could have permitted such a development to grow before his very eyes when by one quick and dexterous strike with a flat-iron it might have been remedied. He would look at the angle of incidence made by the sun's rays on one side of his nose and then at the angle of reflection on the other, and find himself lost in amazement that anything so thin could produce so dark a shadow.

MR. RICKETTY.

It is a most uncomfortable nose. It had a way of hanging protectingly over his heavy dark-brown mustache, which, in its turn, hangs protectingly over his thin, wide lips, so as to make it disagreeably certain that they can open and shut, laugh, snap, and sneer without any one being the wiser.

Upon lines almost parallel with those of his nose, his sharp chin extends out and down, fitting by means of another angle upon his long neck, wherein his Adam's apple, like the corner of a cube, wanders up and down at random. Under his side-whiskers the outlines of his square jaws are faintly to be traced, holding in position a pair of hollow checks that end directly under his eyes in a little knob of ruddy flesh.

Mr. Ricketty is walking along the Bowery. His step is light and easy, and an air pervades him betokening peace and serenity of mind. In one hand he carries a short rattan stick, which he twirls in his fingers carelessly. His little black eyes travel further and faster than his legs, and rove up and down and across the Bowery ceaselessly. He stops in front of a building devoted, according to the signs spread numerously about it, to a variety of trade.

The fifth floor is occupied by a photographer, the fourth by a dealer in picture frames, the third and the second are let out for offices. Over the first hangs the gilded symbol of the three balls and the further information, lettered on a signboard, "Isaac Buxbaum, Money to Loan." The basement is given over to a restaurant-keeper whose identity is fixed by the testimony of another signboard, bearing the two words, "Butter-cake Bob's." Mr. Ricketty's little black eyes wander for an instant up and down the front of the building, and then he trips lightly down the basement steps into the restaurant.

A score or more of small tables fastened securely to the floor—for many, as Bob often said, "comes here deep in liquor an' can't tell a white-pine table from a black felt hat"—were disposed about the room at measured distances from each other, equipped with four short-legged stools, a set of casters, and a jar of sugar, all so firmly fixed as to baffle both cupidity and nervousness. On walls, posts, and pillars were hung a number of allusions to the variety and excellence of Bob's larder.

It was represented that coffee and cakes could be obtained for the trifling sum of ten cents, that corned-beef hash was a specialty, and that as for Bob's chicken soup it was the best in the Bowery. Apparently attracted by this statement, Mr. Ricketty sat down, and intimated to a large young man who presented himself that he was willing to try the chicken soup together with a cup of coffee.

The young man lifted his head and shouted vociferously toward the ceiling, "Chicken in de bowl, draw one!"

"My friend," said Mr. Ricketty, "what a noble pair of lungs you've got and what a fine quality of voice."

The young man grinned cheerfully.

"I am tempted to lavish a cigar on you," continued Mr. Ricketty, "in token of my regard for those lungs. A cigar represents to me a large amount of capital, but it shall all be yours if you'll just step upstairs and see if my old friend, Ike Buxbaum, is in."

"He aint in," said the waiter.

"How do you know?"

"I jist seen him goin' down de street."

"Who runs his business when he adjourns to the street."

"Dunno. Guess it's his wife."

"Aha! the beauteous Becky?"

"I dunno; I've seen a woman in dere."

"You're sure Ike has gone off, are you?"

"Didn't I say I seen him?"

"True. I am answered. My friend, there's the cigar. There, too, are the fifteen cents wherewith to pay for my frugal luncheon. Look upon the luncheon when it comes as yours. I bethink me of an immediate engagement," and rising abruptly Mr. Ricketty hastened out of the restaurant into the street.

"CHICKEN IN DE BOWL, DRAW ONE!"

He glanced quickly through the pawnshop window and made out the figure of a woman standing within among the shadows. He adjusted his hat to his head and a winsome smile to his countenance, and entered.

"Good morning!" he said, breezily, to the young woman who came forward, "where's Ike?"

"Gone out," she answered, looking him over carefully.

"Tut, tut, tut," said Mr. Ricketty, as if utterly annoyed and disappointed. "That's too bad. Will he be gone long?"

"All the morning."

"Will he now? Well, I'll call again," and Mr. Ricketty started for the door. He stopped when he had gone a step or two, however, and, wheeling about, looked earnestly at Becky.

"Let me see," he said, "you must be Ike's wife. You must be the fair and radiant Becky. There's no doubt of it, not the least, now, is there?"

"Well, what if there aint?" said Becky, coolly.

"Why if there aint you ought to know me. You ought to have heard Ike speaking of his friend Ricketty. You ought to have heard him telling of what a good-for-nothing old fool I am. If you are Becky, then you and I are old friends."

"S'posin' we be," said Becky, "what then?"

"To be sure," Mr. Ricketty replied, "what then? Then, Becky, fair daughter of Israel, I've a treasure for you. I always lay my treasure at the feet of my friends. This may not be wise; it may not be the way to grow rich; but it is Steve Ricketty's way, and he can't help it. I have a treasure here now for you. It has taken months of suffering and sorrow to induce me to part with it. Around it cluster memories of other and brighter days. Look!"

Mr. Ricketty produced a string of large and beautiful pearls. They were evidently of the very finest quality, and Becky's black eyes sparkled as she caught their radiance.

"See," said Mr. Ricketty, "see the bedazzling heirloom. Full oft, sweet Jewess, have I held it to my bosom, have I bedewed it with my tears—"

"Oh, yes," interrupted Becky, with a satirical smile, "that's what's made the colors so fine, I suppose."

"Becky, do not taunt me," Mr. Ricketty answered, reproachfully. "This is a sad hour to me. What'll you give for it?"

"Where did it come from?" asked Becky, shrewdly. "We like to know what we're doing when we buy pearl necklaces at retail."

"It was my mother's," replied Mr. Ricketty, touching his handkerchief to his eyes. "When she breathed her last she placed these pearls about my neck. 'Stephen,' she said, 'keep them for my sake.'"

Becky hesitated. Not that she was at all impressed with this story of how the necklace came into Mr. Ricketty's possession. She was fully alive to the risk she ran in entering into any bargain with gentlemen of Mr. Ricketty's appearance, but the luster of the pearls burned in Becky's eyes.

"Well," she said, with a vast assumption of indifference, "I'll give you fifty dollars for them."

Mr. Ricketty cast forth at her one long, scornful look and then started to go out.

"Oh, well," she called after him, "I'll be liberal. I'll make it a hundred."

"No, Becky, you wont. You'll not get that glorious relic for the price of a champagne supper. I will die. I will take my pearls and go and jump off the bridge, and together we'll float with the turning tide out into the blue sea. Adieu, Rebecca, so beautiful and yet so cold, adieu! How could Heaven have made thy face so fair, thine eyes so full of light, thy ruddy lips so merry, but thy heart so hard! I press thy hand for the last time, fair Rebecca—"

"Well, I like that," cried Becky; "seeing that it's the first. You're very gay for a man of your years, and you'd best keep your fine words for them that wants 'em,—*I* don't"; and Becky withdrew her hand, detaining, however, the pearls within it.

Becky was not ill-favored. Her black, silky hair, as fine as a Skye terrier's, curled around a comely head. Her complexion was soft and dark, and her figure light and easy in its movement. These peculiarities, together with her way of fondling the pearls, did not escape Mr. Ricketty's calculating observation.

"Becky," he began blandly.

"Who told you to call me 'Becky'?" she angrily demanded.

"Daughter of Canaan, lend me thine ear, itself as fair as any of these gems of the Southern Sea."

"Oh, come off!" said Becky.

"It has cost me many pangs to bring these jewels here—"

"And you're going to sell them at so much the pang, I s'pose."

"For hours together have I walked up and down the Bowery, trying to rouse my feeble courage. But when I would stop under the three golden balls, I seemed to see a sneer on every passer's lips. They were all saying, 'There goes Steve Ricketty, about to sell his fond mother's pearls.' The thought choked me, Becky, it burned my filial heart."

"Don't seem as if it did your cheek no harm," observed Becky dryly.

"But when I saw your face through the window there, so beautiful and sympathetic, I said to myself, 'There is a true woman. She will feel for me and my grief.' Suppose we make it two hundred and fifty. Come, Becky, the pearls are yours for two hundred and fifty."

"I wont."

"Am I deceived? No, no, it can't be true. I will not believe—"

"I'll tell you what I'll do. I'll give you two hundred to get rid of you."

Mr. Ricketty picked up a little hand-glass that lay upon the counter and placed it before her face.

"Look there," he said, "and tell me what it is that makes Rebecca so heartless. Not those lustrous eyes, so frank and warm; not that—"

"Oh, now, stop that."

"Not that sensitive, shapely nose—"

"Well, I thank goodness it's got no such bulge on it as yours."

"Not those refined lips, arched like the love-god's bow and many times as dangerous; not those cheeks—those soft peach-tinted cheeks, telling in dainty blushes—"

"Oh, six bright stars!"

"Of a soul pure as a sunbeam—"

"Now, I want you to stop and go 'way. I wont take your old pearls at any price."

"Not that brow—that fair, enameled brow—nor yet that creamy throat. Think, sweet Becky, just how these pearls would look clasped with their diamond catch about that creamy throat. I fear to show you lest their luster pale. But yet, I will! See!" and catching up the jewels he threw them about her neck and held the glass steadily before her.

Becky looked. It was evidently not a new idea to Becky. She had all along been considering just the situation Mr. Ricketty proposed, and when he finally dropped the pearls and struck an attitude of profound admiration, Becky snatched the prize from her neck, slid it into a drawer under the counter, and drew a leather purse from the safe behind her. She had begun to count out the money, when a figure passing the window caught her eye.

"There!" she said sharply. "You've been bothering me so long that Ike's come back, and we've got to go through a scene. Two hundred and fifty dollars! It'll break Ike's heart."

Mr. Ricketty snatched the pocket-book from her hands, coolly extracted bills to the amount of two hundred and fifty dollars, returned the book, and whipped out his handkerchief. As the Jew entered he beheld a man leaning against his counter holding a wad of greenbacks in his hand and sobbing violently.

Apparently summoning all his resolution, Mr. Ricketty dried his eyes and fervently grasped the money-lender's hand.

"Ikey, my boy," he said, "I leave my all with you. I go from your door, Ikey, like one who treads alone some banquet hall deserted. I have sold you my birthright, dear boy, for a mess of pottage—a mere mess of pottage—a paltry two hundred and fifty dollars."

Ikey turned pale. "Pecky!" he cried, "who vas der fool mans und vat he means apoudt der dwo huntered und feefty tollars, hey?"

"Well may you call me a fool, Ikey; I can't deny it. I can't even lift my voice in protest. No man in his sober senses would have sold that necklace of glorious gems for such a miserable pittance. Here, Ikey, take back your money and give me my pearls."

BECKY.

He held out the greenbacks with one hand, while with the other he placed his handkerchief to his eyes, of which with great dexterity he reserved a considerable corner for the purposes of observation. At the same time, Becky, well knowing that she had bought the pearls for a sum which, though probably more than her husband would have consented to give, was still far less than their value, handed him the necklace.

The pawnbroker looked from money to jewels and from jewels to money with an expression of curiously mingled grief and greed. Finally, taking Ricketty by the coat-tails, he dragged him towards the door, saying, "I nefer go pack by anydings vat mine vife does, meester, but ven you haf shewels some more, yust coom along ven I vas der shtore py mineselluf, hey?"

Mr. Ricketty shook his hand effusively. "I will, Ikey, I will. These women are very unsatisfactory to deal with. Au revoir, Ikey! Au revoir, madam!" and bowing with the utmost urbanity to the genial Becky, he strode into the street.

It was easy to see, as Mr. Ricketty wandered aimlessly down the Bowery, that his humor was entirely amiable. The knobs of ruddy flesh under his twinkling black eyes were encircled by a set of merry wrinkles, and his mustache had expanded far across his face.

THE PAWNBROKER.

He had gone as far as Canal Street, and was just about to turn the corner, when he heard a low, chirping sort of whistle. All in a second his face changed its expression. The merry wrinkles melted and his mustache drew itself compactly together. But he did not turn his head or alter his gait. He walked on for several steps until he heard the whistle again, and this time its tone was sharp. He stopped, wheeled around, and encountered two men.

One of these was a darkly tinted, strongly built man, with big brown eyes, tremendous arms, and an oppressive manner. To him Mr. Ricketty at once addressed himself.

"Ah, my dear Inspector!" he cried gayly. "I'm amazingly happy to see you. You're looking so well and hearty."

"Yes, Steve," replied the darkly tinted man, "I'm feeling fairly well, Steve, and how is it with you?"

"So, so."

"I haven't happened to meet you recently, Steve."

"Well, no, Inspector. I've been West, but my brother's death—"

"I never knew you had a brother, Steve?"

"Oh, yes, Inspector; and a charming fellow he was. He died last week and—"

"Was he honest, Steve?"

"As honest as a quart measure."

"And did he tell the truth?"

"Like a sun-dial."

"Then it's an almighty pity he died, for you need that kind of man in your family, Steve."

Mr. Ricketty closed one of his little black eyes, and drew down the ends of his mustache, but beyond this indirect method of communicating his thoughts he made no reply to this observation.

"I suppose you're not contemplating a very long stay in the city, Steve?" suggested the Inspector.

"N—n—no," said Mr. Ricketty.

"You seem in doubt?"

"No, I guess I'll return to the West this afternoon."

"Well, on the whole, I shouldn't wonder if that wouldn't be best. Your brother's estate can be settled up, I fancy, without you?"

"It aint very large."

"Well, then, good-by, Steve, and, mind now, this afternoon."

"All right, Inspector; good-by!"

As Mr. Ricketty disappeared down Canal Street, the inspector of police turned to his friend and said: "That fellow was a clergyman once, and they say he used to preach brilliant sermons."

II.

MR. JAYRES.

BOOTSEY BIGGS was a Boy. From the topmost hair of his shocky head to the nethermost sole of his tough little feet, Bootsey Biggs was a Boy. Bootsey was on his way to business. He had come to his tenement home in Cherry Street, just below Franklin Square, to partake of his noonday meal. He had climbed five flights of tenement-house stairs, equal to about thirty flights of civilized stairs, and procuring the key of his mother's room from Mrs. Maguinness, who lived in the third room beyond, where it was always left when Mrs. Biggs went out to get her papers, he had entered within the four walls that he called his home.

Spread upon the little pine table that stood in one corner was his luncheon all ready for him, and after clambering into the big dry-goods box originally purchased for a coal-bin, but converted under the stress of a recent emergency into the baby's crib, and after kissing and poking and mauling and squeezing the poor little baby into a mild convulsion, Bootsey had gone heartily at work upon his luncheon.

He was now satisfied. His stomach was full of boiled cabbage, and his soul was full of peace. He clambered back into the dry-goods box and renewed his guileless operations on the baby. By all odds the baby was the most astonishing thing that had ever come under Bootsey's observation, and the only time during which Bootsey was afforded a fair and uninterrupted opportunity of examining the baby was that period of the day which Mr. Jayres, Bootsey's employer, was wont to term "the noonday hour."

Long before Bootsey came home for his luncheon, Mrs. Biggs was off for her stand in front of "The Sun" building, where she conducted a large and, let us hope, a lucrative business in the afternoon newspapers, so that Bootsey and the baby were left to enjoy the fulness of each other's society alone and undisturbed.

To Bootsey's mind the baby presented a great variety of psychological and other problems. He wondered what could be the mental operation that caused it to kink its nose in that amazing manner, why it should manifest such a persistent desire to swallow its fist, what could be the particular woe and grievance that suddenly possessed its little soul and moved it to pucker up its mouth and yell as though it saw nothing but despair as its earthly portion?

Bootsey had debated these and similar questions until two beats upon the clock warned him that, even upon the most liberal calculation, the noonday hour must be looked upon as gone. Then he rolled the baby up in one corner of the box and started back to the office.

It was Mr. Absalom Jayres's office to which Bootsey's way tended, and a peculiarity about it that had impressed both Mr. Jayres and Bootsey was that Bootsey could perform a given distance of which it was the starting-point in at least one-tenth the time required to perform the same distance of which it was the destination. This was odd, but true.

After taking leave of the baby and locking it in, all snugly smothered at the bottom of its dry-goods box, Bootsey delivered the key of the room to Mrs. Maguinness and descended into the court. Here he found two other boys involved in a difficulty. Things had gone so far that Bootsey saw it would be a waste of time to try to ascertain the merits of the controversy—his only and obvious duty being to hasten the crisis.

"Hi! Shunks!" he cried, "O'll betcher Jakey kin lick ye!"

The rapidity with which this remark was followed by offensive movements on Shunks's part proved how admirably it had been judged.

"Kin he!" screamed Shunks. "He's nawfin' but a Sheeny two-fer!"

Jakey needed no further provocation, and with great dexterity he crowded his fists into Shunks's eyes, deposited his head in Shunks's stomach, and was making a meritorious effort to climb upon Shunks's shoulders, when a lordly embodiment of the law's majesty hove gracefully into sight. Bootsey yelled a shrill warning, and himself set the example of flight.

While passing under the Brooklyn Bridge Bootsey met a couple of Chinamen, and moved by a sudden inspiration he grabbed the cue of one of them, and both he and the Chinaman precipitately sat down. Bootsey recovered quickly and in a voice quivering with rage he demanded to know what the Chinaman had done that for. A large crowd immediately assembled and lent its interest to the solution of this question. It was in vain that the Chinaman protested innocence of any aggressive act or thought. The crowd's sympathies were with Bootsey, and when he insisted that the Mongol had tangled him up in his pig-tail, the aroused populace with great difficulty restrained its desire to demolish the amazed heathens. At last, however, they were permitted to go, followed by a rabble of urchins, and Bootsey proceeded on his way to the office.

HE GRABBED THE CUE OF ONE OF THEM.

Many other interruptions retarded his progress. He had not gone far before he was invited into a game of ball, and this, of course, could not be neglected. The game ending in a general conflict of the players, caused by Bootsey's falling on top of another boy, whom he utterly refused to let up unless it should be admitted that the flattened unfortunate was "out," he issued from the turmoil in time to join in an attack upon a peanut roaster and to avail himself largely of the spoils. Enriched with peanuts, he had got as far as the City Hall Park when a drunken man attracted his attention, and he assisted actively in an effort to convince the drunken man that the Mayor's office was the ferry to Weehawken. It was while engaged in giving these disinterested assurances that he felt himself lifted off his feet by a steady pull at his ears, and looking up he beheld Mr. Jayres.

"You unmitigated little rascal!" cried Mr. Jayres, "where've you been?"

"Nowhere," said Bootsey, in an injured tone.

"Didn't I tell you to get back promptly?"

"Aint I a-getting' back?"

"Aint you a-get—whew!" roared Mr. Jayres, with the utmost exasperation, "how I'd like to tan your plaguey little carcass till it was black and blue! Come on, now," and Mr. Jayres strode angrily ahead.

Bootsey followed. He offered no reply to this savage expression, but from his safe position in the rear he grinned amiably.

Mr. Jayres was large and dark and dirty. His big fat face, shaped like a dumpling, wore a hard and ugly expression. Small black eyes sat under his low, expansive forehead. His cheeks and chin were supposed to be shaven, and perhaps that experience may occasionally have befallen them. His costume was antique. Around his thick neck he wore a soiled choker. His waistcoat was low, and from it protruded the front of a fluted shirt. A dark-blue swallow-tail coat with big buttons and a high collar wrapped his huge body, and over his shoulders hung a heavy mass of black hair, upon which his advanced age had made but a slight impression.

"WE'VE CALLED," SAID THE MAN, SLOWLY.

His office was upon the top floor of a building in Murray Street. It was a long, low room. Upon its door was fastened a battered tin sign showing the words: "Absalom Jayres, Counsellor." The walls and ceiling were covered with dusty cobwebs. In one end of the room stood an old wood stove, and near it was a pile of hickory sticks. A set of shelves occupied a large portion of the wall, bearing many volumes, worn, dusty, and eaten with age.

Among them were books of the English peerage, records of titled families, reports of the Court of Chancery in hundreds of testamentary cases, scrapbooks full of newspaper clippings concerning American claimants to British fortunes, lists of family estates in Great Britain and Ireland, and many other works bearing upon heraldry, the laws of inheritance, and similar subjects.

Upon the walls hung charts showing the genealogical trees of illustrious families, tracing the descent of Washington, of Queen Victoria, and of other important personages. There was no covering on the floor except that which had accumulated by reason of the absence of broom and mop. A couple of tables, a few dilapidated chairs, a pitcher and a basin, were about all the furniture that the room contained.

Being elderly and huge, it required far more time for Mr. Jayres to make the ascent to his office than for Bootsey. Having this fact in mind, Bootsey sat down upon the first step of the first flight, intending to wait until Mr. Jayres had at least reached the final flight before he started up at all. He failed to communicate his resolution, however, and when Mr. Jayres turned about upon the third floor, hearing no footsteps behind him, he stopped. He frowned. He clinched his fist and swore.

"There'll be murder on me," he said, "I know there will, if that Boy don't do better! Now, where the pestering dickens can he be?"

Mr. Jayres leaned over the bannister and started to call. "Boo—" he roared, and then checked himself. "Drat such a name as that," he said. "Who ever heard of a civilized Boy being called Bootsey? What'll people think to see a man of my age hanging over a bannister yelling 'Bootsey'! No, I must go down and hunt him up. I wonder why I keep that Boy? I wonder why I do it?"

Mr. Jayres turned, and with a heavy sigh he began to descend to the street. On the second landing he met Bootsey smoking a cigarette and whistling. Mr. Jayres did not fly into a passion. He did not grow red and frantic. He just took Bootsey by the hand and led him, step by step, up the rest of the way to the office. He drew him inside, shut the door, and led him over to his own table. Then he sat down, still holding Bootsey's hand, and waited until he had caught his breath.

"Now, then," he said, at last.

"Yez'r," said Bootsey.

"You're a miserable little rogue!" said Mr. Jayres.

Bootsey held his peace.

"I've stood your deviltries till I've got no patience left, and now I'm going to discharge you!"

"Aw, don't," said Bootsey.

"Yes," said Mr. Jayres, "I will; if I don't, the end of it all will be murder. Some time or other I'll be seized of a passion, and there's no telling what'll happen. There's your two dollars to the end of the week—now, go!"

"Aw, now," said Bootsey, "wot's de use? I aint done nawfin'. 'Fi gets bounced mom'll drub me awful! You said you wanted me to take a letter up to Harlem dis afternoon."

"Yes, you scamp! And here's the afternoon half gone."

"O'll have it dere in less 'n no time," pleaded Bootsey.

Mr. Jayres scowled hard at Bootsey and hesitated. But finally he drew the letter from the drawer of his table and handed it over, saying as he did so, "If you aint back here by 5 o'clock, I'll break every bone in your body!"

Bootsey left the office with great precipitation, and as he closed the door behind him, Mr. Jayres glared morosely at a knot-hole in the floor. "Funny about that boy!" he said reflectively. "I don't know as I ever gave in to any living human being before that Boy came along in all my life."

Mr. Jayres turned to his table and began to write, but was almost immediately interrupted by a knock upon the door. He called out a summons to enter, and two people, a man and a woman, came in. The man was large, stolid, and rather vacant in his expression. The woman was small and quick and sharp.

"Well, sir," said Mr. Jayres.

The woman poked the man and told him to speak.

"We've called—" said the man slowly.

"About your advertisement in the paper," added the woman quickly.

"Which paper?" asked Mr Jayres.

"Where's the paper?" asked the man, turning to the woman.

"Here," she replied, producing it.

"Oh, yes, I see," said Mr. Jayres, "it's about the Bugwug estate. What is your name, sir?"

"His name is Tobey, and I'm Mrs. Tobey, and we keeps the Gallinipper Laundry, sir, which is in Washington Place, being a very respectable neighborhood, though the prices is low owing to competition of a party across the street."

"Now, Maggie," said the man, "let me talk."

"Who's hindering you from talking, Tobey? I'm not, and that's certain. The gentleman wanted to know who we were, and I've told him. He'd been a week finding out from you."

"Come, come," said Mr. Jayres sharply, "let's get to business."

"That's what I said," replied Mrs. Tobey, "while I was putting on my things to come down town. 'Tobey,' says I, 'get right to business. Don't be wasting the gentleman's time,' which he always does, sir, halting and hesitating and not knowing what to say, nor ever coming to the point. 'It's bad manners,' says I, 'and what's more, these lawyers,' says I, 'which is very sharp folks, wont stand it,' says I. But I don't suppose I done him much good, for he's always been that way, sir, though I'm sure I've worked my best to spur him up. But a poor, weak woman can't do everything, though you'd think he thought so, if—"

"Oh, now stop, stop, stop!" cried Mr. Jayres, "you mustn't run on so. Your name is Tobey and you have called about the Bugwug property. Well, now, what of it?"

"I want to know is there any money in it," answered Mr. Tobey.

"Now, if you please, sir, just listen to that," cried Mrs. Tobey pityingly. "He wants to know is there money in it! Why, of course, there's money in it, Tobey. You're a dreadful trial to me, Tobey. Didn't the gentleman's advertisement say there was 500,000 pounds in it? Aint that enough? Couldn't you and me get along on 500,000 pounds, or even less, on a pinch?"

"But the question is," said Mr. Jayres, "what claim you have on the Bugwug property. Are you descended from Timothy Bugwug, and if so, how directly and in what remove?"

"That's what we wants you to tell us, sir," replied Mr. Tobey.

"Why, we supposed you'd have it all settled," added his wife. "Aint you a lawyer?"

"Oh, yes, I'm a lawyer," Mr. Jayres suavely replied, "and I can tell you what your claim is if I know your relationship to Timothy Bugwug. He died in 1672, leaving four children, Obediah, Martin, Ezekiel, and Sarah. Obediah died without issue. Martin and Sarah came to America, and Ezekiel was lost at sea before he had married. Now then, where do you come in?"

"My mother—" said Mr. Tobey.

"Was a Bugwug," said Mrs. Tobey. "There's no doubt at all but what all that money belongs to us, and if you've got it you must pay it right away to us, for plenty of use we have for it with six young children a-growing up and prospects of another come April, which as regards me is terrible to think of, though, I suppose, I shouldn't repine, seeing that it's the Lord's will that woman should suffer, which, I must say, it seems to me that they have more than their fair share. However, I don't blame Tobey, for he's a fine man, and a hard-working one, if he hasn't got the gift of speech and is never able to come to the point, though that's not for the lack of having it dinged into his ears, for if I says it once I says it fifty times a day, 'Tobey, will you come to the point?'"

Mr. Jayres took up his pen. "Well, let's see," he said. "What is your full name, Mr. Tobey?"

"William Tobey, sir. I am the son of—"

"Jonathan Tobey and Henrietta Bugwug," continued the lady, "it being so stated in the marriage license which the minister said was for my protection, and bears the likeness of Tobey on one side and mine on the other and clasped hands in the center signifying union, and is now in the left-hand corner of the sixth shelf from the bottom in the china closet and can be produced at any time if it's needful. I've kept it very careful."

"Whose daughter was Henrietta Bugwug?" asked Mr. Jayres.

"Tobey's grandfather's, sir, a very odd old gentleman, though blind, which he got from setting off fireworks on a Fourth of July, and nearly burned the foot off the blue twin, called blue from the color of his eyes, the other being dark-blue, which is the only way we have of telling 'em apart, except that one likes cod liver oil and the other don't, and several times when the blue twin's been sick the dark-blue twin has got all the medicine by squinting up his eyes so as I couldn't make him out and pretending it was him that had the colic, and Mr. Bugwug, that's Tobey's grandfather, lives in Harlem all by himself, because he says there's too much noise and talking in our flat, and I dare say there is, though I don't notice it."

"In Harlem, eh? When did you first hear that you had an interest in the Bugwug estates?"

"Oh, ever so long, and we'd have had the money long ago if it hadn't been that a church burned down a long time ago somewhere in Virginia where one of the Bugwugs married somebody and all the records were lost, though I don't see what that had to do with it, because Tobey's here all ready to take the property, and it stands to reason that he wouldn't have been here unless that wedding had 'a' happened without they mean to insult us, which they'd better not, and wont, if they know when they are well off," and at the very thought of such a thing Mrs. Tobey tossed her head angrily.

"I see," said Mr. Jayres, "I see. And you want me to take the matter in hand, I suppose, and see if I can recover the money, eh?"

"Oh, dear!" said Mrs. Tobey, in a disappointed tone, "I thought from the piece in the paper that the money was all ready for us."

"You mustn't be so impatient," soothingly responded Mr. Jayres, laying his fat finger on his fat cheek and smiling softly. "All in good time. All in good time. The money's where it's safe. You only need to establish your right to it. We must fetch a suit in the Court of Chancery, and that I'll do at once upon looking up the facts. Of course—er—there'll be a little fee."

"A little what?" said Mr. Tobey.

"A little which?" said Mrs. Tobey.

"A LITTLE FEE," SAID MR. JAYRES, SMILING SWEETLY.

"A little fee," said Mr. Jayres, smiling sweetly. "A mere trifle, I assure you; just enough to defray expenses—say—er—a hundred dollars."

"Oh, dear me!" cried Mrs. Tobey. "This is vexing. To think of coming down town, Tobey, dear, with the expectations of going back rich, and then going back a hundred dollars poorer than we were. I really don't think we'd better do it, Tobey?"

"Ah," said Mr. Jayres, "but think also of the fortune. Two millions and a half! Isn't that worth spending a few hundred dollars for? Just put your mind on it, ma'am."

"I've had my mind on it ever since I seen your piece in the paper," replied Mrs. Tobey, "and a hundred dollars does seem, as you say, little enough to pay for two millions and a half, which would be all I'd ask or wish for, and would put us where we belong, Tobey, which is not in the laundry line competing with an unscrupulous party across the street, though I don't mention names, which perhaps I ought, for the public ought to be warned. It's a party that hasn't any honor at all—"

"I'm sure not," said Mr. Jayres sympathetically. "He is, without doubt, a dirty dog."

"Oh, it isn't a he," Mrs. Tobey replied, "the party is a her."

"THE PARTY IS A HER," SAID MRS. TOBEY.

"Of course, of course," said Mr. Jayres. "And to think that you have to put up with the tricks of a female party directly across the street. Why, it's shameful, ma'am! But if you had that two millions, as you just observed, all that would be over."

"Two million and a half I thought you said it was," said Mrs. Tobey rather sharply.

"Oh, yes, and a half—and a half," the lawyer admitted in a tone of indifference, as much as to say that there should be no haggling about the odd $500,000. "What a pretty pile it is, Mrs. Tobey?"

"I don't know, Tobey, but what we'd better do it," Mrs. Tobey said after a pause. "It aint so very much when you think of what we're to get for it."

"That's the right way to look at it, ma'am. I'll just draw up the receipt, and to-morrow I'll call at the Gallinipper Laundry to get some further particulars necessary to help me make out the papers."

Mr. Tobey seemed to be somewhat at a loss to know precisely what was the net result of the proceedings in which he had thus far taken so small a part, but upon being directed by Mrs. Tobey to produce the hundred dollars, he ventured a feeble remonstrance. This was immediately checked by Mrs. Tobey, who assured him that he knew nothing whatever about such matters and never could come to the point, which he ought to be able to do by this time, for nobody could say but that she had done her part. At last two fifty-dollar bills were deposited in Mr. Jayres's soft palm and a bit of writing was handed over to Mrs. Tobey in exchange for them; and followed by Mr. Jayres's warm insistence that they had never done a better thing in their lives, the Tobeys withdrew.

It was nearly six o'clock when the door of Mr. Jayres's office opened again and the shocky head of Bootsey appeared. Mr. Jayres was waiting for him.

"Here you are at last, you wretched little scamp!" he cried. "Didn't I tell you I'd whale you if you weren't back by five o'clock?"

"I come jest as soon 's I could," said Bootsey. "He was a werry fly ole gen'l'man."

"What did he say?"

"He said he didn't hev no doubts but wot you was a reg'lar villyum an' swin'ler, an' cheat an' blackmailer, an' ef he had de user his eyes an' legs he'd come down yere an' han' you over ter de coppers; dat you aint smart enuff ter get no money outer him, fer he's bin bled by sich coveys like you all he's a-going ter bleed, an' dat he don't b'lieve dere is any sech ting as de Bugwug estate nohow, an' ef yer wants ter keep outen jail yer'd better let him an' his folks alone."

Mr. Jayres scowled until it seemed as if his black eyebrows would meet his bristly upper lip, and then he said: "Bootsey, before you come to the office to-morrow morning you'd better go to the Gallinipper Laundry in Washington Place, and tell a man named Tobey who keeps it, that—er—that I've gone out of town for a few days, Bootsey, on a pressing matter of business."

III.

BLUDOFFSKI.

The friends of Mr. Richard O'Royster always maintained that he was the best of good fellows. Many, indeed, went so far as to say he had no faults whatever; and while such an encomium seems, on the face of it, to be extravagant, its probability is much strengthened by the fact that whatever he had they always came into the possession of sooner or later. If he had any faults, therefore, they must have known it. They would never have allowed anything so valuable as a fault to escape them.

Mr. O'Royster was sitting, one afternoon, in the private office of his bankers, Coldpin & Breaker. Mr. Coldpin sat with him, discussing the advisability of his investing $250,000 in the bonds of the East and West Telegraph Company. It was a safe investment, in Mr. Coldpin's judgment, and Mr. O'Royster was about to order the transaction carried out, when the office door was thrust open and a long, black-bearded, wiry-haired, savage-looking man walked in.

BLUDOFFSKI.

His head was an irregular hump set fixedly on his shoulders so that one almost expected to hear it creak when he moved it. His eyes were little, and curiously stuck on either side of his thick, stumpy nose, as if it were only by the merest accident that they hadn't taken a position back of his ears or up in his forehead or down in his hollow cheeks. His entrance put a sudden and disagreeable stop to the conversation. Mr. O'Royster adjusted his eyeglass and looked with a sort of serene curiosity at the man. Mr. Coldpin moved nervously in his chair.

"Vell," the fellow said, after a pause, "I haf come to sbeak mit you."

"You come very often," replied Mr. Coldpin in a mildly remonstrative tone.

No answer was returned to this suggestion. The intruder simply settled himself on his feet in an obstinate sort of way.

Mr. Coldpin produced a dollar-bill and handed it over, remarking testily, "There, now, I'm very busy!"

"Nein, nein!" said the man. "It vas not enough!"

"Not enough?"

"I vants dwenty tollar."

"Oh, come now; this wont do at all. You mustn't bother me so. I can't be——"

The man did something with his mouth. Possibly he smiled. Possibly he was malevolently disposed. At all events, whatever his motive or his humor, he did something with his mouth, and straightway his two rows of teeth gleamed forth, his eyes changed their position and also their hue, and the hollows in his cheeks became caverns.

"Great Cæsar!" cried Mr. O'Royster. "Look here, my good fellow, now don't! If you must have the money, we'll try to raise it. Don't do that. Take in your teeth, my man, take 'em in right away, and we'll see what we can do about the twenty."

He composed his mouth, reducing it to its normal dimensions and arranging it in its normal shape, whereupon Mr. O'Royster, drawing a roll of bills from his pocket, counted out twenty dollars.

Mr. Coldpin interposed. "You may naturally think, O'Royster," he observed quietly, "that this man has some hold upon me by which he is in a position to extort money. There is no such phase to this remarkable case. I owe him nothing. He is simply in the habit of coming here and demanding money, which I have let him have from time to time in small sums to—well, get rid of him. I think, though, that it's time to stop. You must not give him that $20. I won't permit it. Put it back in——"

"IT WOULDN'T HURT HIM TO SHOOT HIM."

The man did something else in a facial way just as defiant of analysis as his previous contortion and equally effective on Mr. O'Royster's nerves. He moved toward Mr. O'Royster and held up his hand for the money. It was slowly yielded up, and without so much as an acknowledgment, the man thrust it into his pocket and stalked out.

Mr. O'Royster watched his misshapen body as it disappeared through the entry. Then he gazed at the banker and finally remarked: "Can't say that your friend pleases me, Coldpin."

"To tell the truth, O'Royster, I live in mortal terror of that creature. He followed me into this room from the street one day and demanded, rather than begged, some money. I scarcely noticed him, telling him I had nothing, when he did something that attracted my attention, and the next minute my flesh began to creep, my backbone began to shake, and I thought I should have spasms. I gave him a handful of change and off he went. Since then, as I told you, he has been coming here every month or so. I'm going to move next May into a building where I can have a more guarded office."

"Odd tale!" said Mr. O'Royster, "deuced odd. Why don't you get a pistol?"

"Well, I have a sort of feeling that it wouldn't hurt him to shoot him. Of course it would, you know, but still—"

"Yes, I know what you mean. He certainly does look as if a pistol would be no adequate defense against him. What you want is a nice, self-cocking, automatic thunderbolt."

They changed the subject, returning to their interrupted business, and having concluded that they talked on until it had grown quite late.

"By Jove!" cried Mr. O'Royster, glancing at his watch, "it's half-past six, and I've a dinner engagement at the club at seven. I must be off. Ring for a cab, wont you?"

The cab arrived in a few moments and Mr. O'Royster hurried out. "Drive me to the Union Club," he said, "and whip up lively."

He sprang in, the cab started off with a whirl, and he turned in his seat to let down the window. A startled look came into his face.

"It's too dark to see well," he said to himself, "and this thing bounces like a tugboat in a gale, but if that ourang-outang wasn't standing under that gaslight yonder, I'll be hanged!"

Mr. O'Royster's was the sort of mind that dwelt lightly and briefly on subjects affecting it disagreeably, and long before he reached the club it had left the ourang-outang far in the distance. In the presence of a jolly company, red-headed duck, burgundy and champagne, it had room for nothing but wit and frolic, to which its inclinations always strongly tended.

The night had far advanced when Mr. O'Royster left the club. He turned into Fifth Avenue, journeying toward Twenty-third Street, and had walked about half the distance when he felt a touch upon his arm. Mr. O'Royster was in that condition when his mental senses acted more quickly than his physical senses. Bringing his eyes to bear upon the spot where he felt the touch, he made out the shape of a big, dirty hand, and following it and the arm above it, he presently ascertained that a man was close at his elbow. He spent several minutes scrutinizing the man's face, and finally he said:

"Ah, I shee. Beg pawdon, dear boy, f'not 'bsherving you b'fore. Mos' happy to renew zhe 'quaintance so auspishously begun 'saffer-noon. H—hic!—'ope you're feeling well. By zhe way, ol' f'llaw, wha' zhure name?"

"Bludoffski."

"Razzer hard name t' pronounce, but easy one t' 'member. Glad 'tain't Dobbins. 'F zenny sing I hate, 's name like Dobb'ns, 'r Wobb'ns, 'r Wigg'ns. Some-pin highly unconventional in name of Bludoffski. Mr. Bludoffski, kindly 'cept 'shurances of my—rhic!—gard!"

Mr. Bludoffski executed a facial maneuver intended possibly for a smile. It excited Mr. O'Royster's attention directly.

"Doffski!" he said, stopping shortly and balancing himself on his legs, "are you sure you're feelin' quite well?"

"Yah, puty vell."

"Zere's no great sorrer gnawin' chure vitals, is zere, Moffski?"

"I vas all ride."

"Not sufferin' f'om any mad r'gret, 'r misplaced love, 'rensing zat kind, eh, Woffski?"

"No."

"Feeling jush sames' ushyal?"

"Yah."

"Zen 'sall right. Don't 'pol'gize, 's all right. Zere was somepin' 'n you're looksh made me shink p'raps yu's feeling trifle in'sposed. I am, an' didn't know but what you might be same way. You may've noticed 't I'm jush trifle—er, well, some people ud shay zhrunk, Toffski—rude 'n' dish'gree'ble people dshay zhrunk. P'raps zere 'bout half right, Woffski, but it's zhrude way of putting it. Now, zhen, I want t'ask you queshun. I ask ash frien'. Look 't me carefully and shay, on y'r honor, Loffski, where d'you shin' I'm mos' largely 'tossicated?"

"In der legs," replied Mr. Bludoffski, promptly.

"Shank you. 'S very kind. 'T may not be alt'gesser dignified to be 'tossicated in zhe legs, but 's far besser'n if 'twas in zhe eyes. 'Spise a man 'at looks drunk in's eyes. Pos'ively 'sgusting!"

They had now reached Twenty-third Street, and following his companion's lead, O'Royster crossed unsteadily into Madison Square and through one of the park walks. Presently he halted.

"By zhe way, Woffski," he said, "do you know where we're goin'?"

"Yah."

"Well, zat's what I call lucky. I'm free t' confesh I haven't gotter shingle idea. But 'f you know, 's all right. W'en a man feels himself slightly 'tossicated, 's nozzin' like bein' in comp'ny of f'law 'at knows where 's goin'. 'Parts a highly 'gree'ble feelin' 'f conf'dence. Don't wanter 'splay any 'pert'nent cur'osity, Boffski, but p'raps 's no harm in askin' where 'tis 'at you know you're goin'?"

"Home."

An expression of disgust crossed Mr. O'Royster's face. "Home?" he inquired. "D' you shay 'home,' Toffski? Haven't you got any uzzer place t' go? Wen a man'sh r'duced t' th' 'str—hic—remity 'f goin' home, must be in dev'lish hard luck."

"Der vhy 've go home," said Bludoffski, "is dot I somedings haf I show you."

"Ah. I shee. Za's diff'rent zing. You're goin' t'show me some-'zin', eh?"

"Yah."

"Picshur? Hope 'taint pichshur, Koffski. I'm ord'narily very fon' of art, but f'law needs good legs t' 'zamine picshur, an' I'm boun'ter confesh my legsh not just 'dapted t'—"

"Nein."

"Eh?"

"It vasn't noddings like dot."

"'Taint china, is 't, Boffski? 'Taint Willow Pattern er Crown Derby er zat sorter zing? T' tell truth, Boffski, I aint mush on china. Some people go crashy at er shight er piece nicked china. My wife tol' me zuzzer day she saw piece Crown Derby 'n' fainted dead way, 'n' r'fused t' come to f'r half 'n hour. I said I'd give ton er Crown Derby for bashket champagne 'n' she didn't speak to me rester 'zhe week. Jush shows how shum people—"

"Nein!"

"Eh?"

"It vasn't shina."

"By zhove, you 'rouse my cur'os'ty, Woffski. If 'tain't picshur er piece pottery, wha' deuce is't?"

"You shall see."

"Myst'ry! Well, I'm great boy f'r myst'ries. Hullo! Zis, zh' place?"

They had walked through Twenty-ninth Street, into Second Avenue, and had reached the center of a gloomy and dismal block. Directly in front of the gloomiest and most dismal house of all Bludoffski had suddenly stopped, and in answer to Mr. O'Royster's exclamation, he drew from his pocket a latch-key and opened the side door.

The entry was dark, but the glimmer of a light was visible at the end of the hall. He did not speak, but motioned with his hand an invitation for Mr. O'Royster to go in. It was accepted, not, however, without a slight manifestation of reluctance. Mr. O'Royster's senses were somewhat clouded, but the shadows of the entry were dark enough to impress even him with a vague feeling of dread.

Bludoffski shut the door behind them carefully and drew a bolt or two. Then he led the way down the hall toward the light. As they advanced voices were heard, one louder than the rest, which broke out in rude interruption, dying down into a sort of murmuring accompaniment.

When they reached the end of the hall Bludoffski opened another door and they entered a large beer saloon. At a score of tables men were sitting, many apparently of German birth. They were smoking pipes, drinking beer, and listening to the hoarse voice of an orator standing in the furthest corner of the room.

He was a little round man with little round eyes, a little round nose, a little round stomach, and little round legs. Though very small in person, his voice was formidable enough, and he appeared to be astonishingly in earnest.

Bludoffski's entrance created a considerable stir. Several persons began to applaud, and some said, "Bravo! bravo!" One sharp-visaged and angular man with black finger-nails, spectacles, and a high tenor voice, cried out with a burst of enthusiasm, "Hail! Dear apostle uf luf!" a sentiment that brought out a general and spontaneous cheer. Mr. O'Royster, apparently under the impression that he was the object of these flattering attentions, bowed and smiled with the greatest cheerfulness and murmured something about this being the proudest moment of his life. He was on the point of addressing some remarks to the bartender, when the little round orator cut in with an energy quite amazing.

"VE VILL SHTRIKE, MEIN PRUDERS!"

"Der zoshul refolushun haf gome, my prudders!" he said. "Der bowder vas all retty der match to be struck mit. Ve neet noddings but ter stretch out mit der hant und der victory dake. Der gabitalist fool himselluf. He say mit himselluf 'I haf der golt und der bower, hey?' He von pig fool. He dinks you der fool vas, und der eye uf him he vinks like der glown py der circus. But yust vait. Vait till der honest sons uf doil rise by deir might oop und smite der blow vich gif liperty to der millions!"

At this there was a wild outburst of applause and a chorus of hoarse shouts: "Up mit der red flag!" "Strike now!" "Anarchy foreffer!"

"Ve vill shtrike, mine prudders," continued the little round orator, growing very ardent and red in the face. "Ve vill no vait long. Ve vill kill! Ve vill burn! Ve vill der togs uf var loose und ride to driumph in der shariot uf fire. Ve vill deir housen pull down deir hets upoud, und der street will run mit der foul plood uf der gabitalist!"

A mighty uproar arose at these gory suggestions, and would not be subdued until all the glasses had been refilled and the enthusiasm that had been aroused was quenched in beer.

Mr. O'Royster had listened to these proceedings with some misgivings. He turned to his companion, who stood solemn and silent by his side, and observed:

"D' I unnerstan' you t' say, Woffski, 't you 's goin' home?"

"Yah."

"Doncher zhink 's mos' time t' go?"

"Ve vas dere now."

"Home?"

"Yah."

"Can't say I'm pleased with your d'mestic surroundings, Boffski. Razzer too mush noise f' man of my temp'ment. Guesh I'll haffer bid you g'night, Boffski."

"Nein."

"Yesh, Boffski, mush go. Gotter 'gagement."

"Vait. I haf not show you yet—"

"T' tell truf, Moffski, I've seen 'nuff. 'F I wasser shee more, might not sleep well. Might have nightmare. Don't shink 's good f' me t' shee too much, ol' f'law."

"Listen."

The little round orator, refreshed and reinvigorated, began again.

"You must arm yoursellef, my prudders. You must haf guns und powder und ball und—"

"Dynamite!" yelled several.

"Yah. Dot vas der drue veapon uf der zoshul refolushun. Dynamite! You must plenty haf. Ve must avenge der murder uf our brudders in Shegaco. Deir innocent plood gries ter heffen for revensh. A t'ousan' lifes vill not der benalty bay. Der goundry must pe drench mit plood. Den vill Anarchy reign subreme ofer de gabitalist vampire! Are you retty?"

The whole crowd rose in a body, banged their glasses viciously on the tables in front of them and shouted: "Ve vas!"

"Den lose no time to rouse your frients. Vake up der laporing mans all eferywhere. Gif dem blenty pomb und der sicnal vatch for, und ven it vas gif shoot und kill und spare nopoddy! Der time for vorts vas gone. Now der time vas for teets!"

"Loffski," whispered Mr. O'Royster, "really must 'scuse me, Loffski, but 's time er go. I have sorter feelin' 's if I's gettin' 'tossercated in zhe eyes. Always know 's time er go when I have zat feelin'. F' I'd know chure home 's in place like zis I'd asked you t' go t' mine where zere's more r—hic—pose."

There was a door behind them near the bar, and Bludoffski, opening it, motioned Mr. O'Royster to go in ahead. He obeyed, not without reluctance, and the Anarchist followed. Two tables covered with papers, a bed and several chairs were in the room, together with many little jars, bits of gaspipe, lumps of sulphur, phosphorus and lead.

"Sit down," said Bludoffski.

Mr. O'Royster sat.

"I am an Anarchist," Bludoffski began.

"'S very nice," Mr. O'Royster replied. "I 's zhinkin' uzzer day 'bout bein' Anarchis' m'self, but Mrs. O'Royster said she's 'fraid m' health washn't good 'nuff f' such—hic—heavy work."

"You hear der vorts uf dot shbeaker und you see der faces uf der men. Vat you t'ink it mean? Hey? It mean var upon der reech. It mean Nye Yorick in ashes—"

"Wha's use? Don't seem t' me s' t' would pay. Of course, ol' f'law, whatever you says, goes. But 't seems t' me—"

"You can safe all dot var. You can der means be uf pringing aboud der reign uf anarchy mitout der shtrike uf von blow. Eferypody vill lif und pe habby."

"Boffski," said Mr. O'Royster, after a pause, during which he seemed to be making a violent effort to gather his intellectual forces. "Zere's no doubt I'm 'tossercated in zhe eyes. W'en a man's eyes 'fected by champagne, he's liter'ly no good. Talk to me 'bout zis t'mor', Woffski. Subjec's too 'mportant to be d'scussed unner present conditions."

"Nein! nein! You can safe der vorlt uf you vill. Von vort from you vill mean peace. Midoutdt dot vort oceans of plood vill be spill."

"Woffski, you ev'dently zhink I zhrunker'n I am. I'm some zhrunk, Woffski, I know, *some* zhrunk, but 'taint 's bad's you zhink."

"I vill sbeak more blain."

"Do, ol' f'law, 'f you please."

"It vas selfishness vot der vorld make pad. It was being ignorant und selfish vot crime und bofferty pring to der many und vealth und ease to der few. Der beoples tondt see dot. Tey tondt know vot Anarchy mean. It vas all rest, all peace, nopoddy pad, no var, no bestilence. Dot is Anarchy, hey?

"I haf my life gif to der cause uf Anarchy. I haf dravel der vorlt over shbeaking, wriding, delling der beoples to make vay for der zoshul refolushun. Uf dey vill not, ve must der reech kill. We must remofe dem vich stand py der roat und stay der march of civilization. Some say 'Make haste! kill! kill!' I say, 'Nein, vait, gif der wretched beoples some chance to be safe. Tell dem vot is Anarchy. Etjucade dem.'

"Vell, den, dey listen to me. Dey say, 'Ve bow der vill before uf Herr Bludoffski, whose vordt vas goot. Ve vait. But how long? Ah, dat I can not tell. But I have decide I make von appeal. I gif der vorlt von chance to come ofer to Anarchy and be save. Ha! Se! I haf write a pook! I haf say der pook inside all apout Anarchy. I haf tell der peauties of der commune, vere no selfishness vas, no law, but efery man equal und none petter as some udder. I haf describe it all. Nopody can dot pook reat mitout he say ven he lay him down, 'I vil be an Anarchist.'"

Mr. Bludoffski had become intensely interested in his own remarks. He picked his manuscripts from the table and caressed them lovingly.

"See," he said, "dere vas der pook vich make mankind brudders. I tell you how you help. I vas poor. I haf no money. I lif on noddings, und dem noddings I peg. Ven I see you und you dot money gif me, I say 'Dis man he haf soul! He shall be save.' Den I say more as dot. I say he shall join his hand mit me. He shall print him, den million copies, send him de vorlt ofer, in all der lankviches, to all der peoples. Dink uf dot! You shall be great Anarchist as I. Ve go down mit fame togedder!"

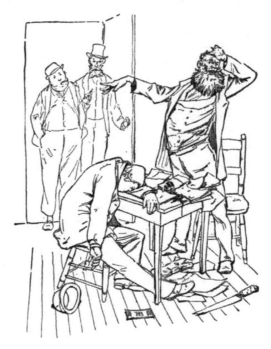

"HE HAF NO SOUL, NO HEART, NO MIND, NO NODDINGS."

He paused for Mr. O'Royster's reply, trembling with fanatical excitement. The reply was somewhat slow in coming. Mr. O'Royster, when his companion began to talk, had leaned his head on his arm and closed his eyes. He had preserved this attitude throughout the address and was now breathing hard.

"Vell!" said Bludoffski, impatiently.

Mr. O'Royster drew a more resonant breath, long, deep and mellow.

"He sleep!" cried Bludoffski, in scornful fury. "Der tog! He sleep ven I tell him—"

He sprang up, ran across the room and returned with a huge carving-knife. "I vill kill him!" he cried, and, indeed, made start to do it. But as suddenly he checked himself, tossed the knife on the floor, muttering, "Bah, he not fit to kill," and opened the door into the saloon. The Anarchist meeting had ended, but several persons were still sitting around the tables, drinking beer. He called to two of these, and said, in a tone of almost pitiful despair:

"Take dot man home. I not know who he vas. I not know vere he lif. Somebotty fin' oud. Look his pockets insite. Ask der boleecemans. Do any dings, but take him avay. He haf no soul, no mind, no heart, no noddings!"

IV.

MAGGIE.

Wrapped in contemplation and but little else, probably because his stock of contemplation largely exceeded his stock of else, Mr. Dootleby wandered down the Bowery. Midnight sounded out from the spire in St. Mark's Church just as Mr. Dootleby, having come from Broadway through Astor Place, turned about at the Cooper Union.

There was a touch of melancholy in Mr. Dootleby's expression as he looked down the big, brilliant Bowery, glowing with the light of a hundred electric burners and myriads of gas-jets, and seething with unnatural activity. He stopped a moment in the shadow thrown by the booth of a coffee and cake vender, and looked attentively into the faces of the throngs that passed him. He seemed to be thinking hard.

MR. DOOTLEBY.

In truth, it is a suggestive place, is the Bowery. Day and night are all the same to it. It never gets up and it never goes to bed. It never takes a holiday. It never keeps Lent. It indulges in no sentiments. It acknowl-edges no authority that bids it remember the Sabbath Day to keep it holy. But from year's end to year's end it bubbles, and boils, and seethes, and frets while the daylight lasts, and in the glare of its brighter night it plunges headlong into carousal!

Mr. Dootleby had a great habit of walking at night, though he seldom came down town so far as this. His apartments were in Harlem, and usually, after he had taken his dinner and played a rubber of whist, he found himself sufficiently exercised by a stroll as far as Forty-second Street. But to-night he felt a trifle restless, and journeyed on.

Though his hair was nearly white and his face somewhat deeply furrowed, Mr. Dootleby's tall heavy figure stood straight toward the zenith, and moved with an ease and celerity that many a younger man had envied. With his antecedents I am not entirely familiar, but they say he was always eccentric. I, for my part, shall like him none the less for this. They say he was rich once, but that he never knew how to take care of his money, and what part of it he did not give away slipped off of its own accord.

They say he was past fifty when he married, and his bride was a young woman, and when they went off together he was as frisky as a young fellow of twenty-three. Then, they say, she died, and after that he took but little interest in things, spending his time chiefly in such amiable pursuits as the entertainment of the children playing in Central Park, and the writing of an occasional article for the scientific papers, on "The Peculiar Behavior of Alloys."

Despite the dinginess of his costume, Mr. Dootleby was a handsome old man, and he looked very out of place on the Bowery. Not that good looks are wanting in the Bowery, for many a crownless Cleopatra mingles with its crowds. But Mr. Dootleby, as he stood in the shadow of the coffee-vender's booth, seemed to be the one kind of being necessarily incongruous with the midnight Bowery spectacle.

Mr. Dootleby stood and looked for full twenty minutes. In some of the faces that passed him he saw only a careless sensuality brightened by the flush of excitement. Others, somewhat older, were full of brazen coarseness, and others, older still, bore that pitiful look of hopeless regret, quickly changing to one that says as plainly as can be that the time for thinking and caring has gone. Upon many was stamped the brand of inborn infamy, their only inheritance.

THE BOWERY NIGHT-SCENE.

Some hunted souls went by, their manner jaded and hapless, their steps
nervous and irresolute, and their eyes sweeping the streets before them,
never resting, never closed. A few as they passed scowled at him—even at
him, as if there were not one in all this world upon whom they had not
declared war. Want had marked most of them with unmistakable lines, and
crossing these were often others telling that they knew no better than they
did.

Mr. Dootleby watched awhile and then went on, pausing occasionally at the
corners to peer through the dark side streets, up at the big tenement-
houses—those ugly nurseries of vice—from whose black shadows came
many of these that had been christened into crime. But in the Bowery itself
there was no gloomy spot. Light streamed from every window, and flooded
the pavements. The street-cars whirled along. Even the bony creatures that
drew them caught the spirit of this feverish thoroughfare. From every other
doorway, shielded by cloth or wicker screens, came the sounds of twanging
harps and scraping fiddles, the click of glasses and the shrill chatter and
laughter of discordant voices.

Here and there, in front of a bewildering canvas, upon which, in the gayest
of gay colors, mountainous fat women, prodigious giants, scaly mermaids,

wild men from Zululand, living skeletons, and three-headed girls were painted, stood clamorous gentlemen in tights, urgently importuning passers-by to enter the establishments they represented, whereof the glories and mysteries could be but too feebly told in words. And upon the sidewalks all about him, swarms of itinerant musicians, instantaneous photographers, dealers in bric-a-brac, toilet articles, precious stones, soda water, and other needful and nutritious wares, urged themselves upon Mr. Dootleby's attention.

He walked leisurely on, moralizing as he went, until he had passed Chatham Square, and had got into the somberer district below. He turned a corner somewhere, thinking to walk around the block and find his way back into the Bowery. But the more corners he rounded the more he found ever at his elbow, and the conviction began to make its way into his mind that he had lost his bearings.

The block in which he was now wandering was quite dark and dismal, save for a single gas-jet hanging almost hidden within a dirty globe, over some steep steps that led into a cellar. Mr. Dootleby concluded to stop there and ask his way. As he approached the cellar, he heard what seemed to be cries of distress. They grew more distinct, and accompanying them were the dull sounds of blows and the harsh accents of a man's voice, evidently permeated with rage.

Mr. Dootleby ran down the steps and flung the door open, presenting his eyes with a spectacle that made his blood run cold. The room was long and narrow. At one end and near the door was a bar fitted up with a few black bottles and broken tumblers, a keg or two of beer, and some boxes of cigars. Along the walls stood a couple of benches, and further on were half a dozen little rooms, partitioned from each other, all opening into the bar-room. On the benches six girls were lolling about, dressed in gaudy tights, and with them were three or four men. The room was hot to suffocation, and the smell from the dim and dirty lamps that stood on each end of the bar, together with the foul tobacco-smoke with which the atmosphere was saturated, combined to make the place disgusting and poisonous.

All these conditions Mr. Dootleby took in at his first glance, and his second fell upon two figures in the center of the room, from whom had proceded the noises he had heard. One was that of a girl cowering on her knees and moaning in a voice from which reason had clearly departed. A big, unconscionably brutal-looking man stood over her, holding her down by her hair, which, braided in a single plait, was wound about his hand. He had just thrown the stick upon the floor with which he had been beating her, and was drawing from the stove a red-hot poker.

THE FELLOW WHEELED QUICKLY AROUND.

Mr. Dootleby was not of an excitable temperament ordinarily, but his senses were so affected by the horrors he saw and the pestilential air he breathed that his head began to swim, and only by an especial draft upon his resolution was he able to command himself. There was a pause consequent upon his entrance, and his quick eyes made good use of it.

He saw that the girl had already been half murdered, and that her assailant was a short, thick-set old man, with the eyes of a snake and the neck of a bull. He saw that the men on the bench, all beastly specimens, were contemplating her torture with an indifference that would have shamed the grossest savage. Several of the women, too—the older ones—were looking on with scarcely the sign of a protest in their faces, and only one, a mere child, seemed to feel a genuine sense of terror and sympathy.

Mr. Dootleby threw open his coat, tightened his grasp on his walking-stick, and said, very quietly: "What are you doing?"

The fellow wheeled quickly around. He looked with intense malice at Mr. Dootleby, and then shouted at one of the women, "Why didencher lock de door like I toljer, you fool?"

Mr. Dootleby did not wait for either of these questions to be answered. He sprang into action with all the agility and ferocity of a young panther. The handle of his cane was a huge knob of carved ivory. He brought it directly on the head of the ruffian in a blow of tremendous force, and as the fellow staggered, Mr. Dootleby grasped the poker, turning it so that its heated end touched his antagonist's arm. Of course, the man loosened his hold, and in an instant more dropped upon the floor. Then Mr. Dootleby, keenly alive to the necessity of improving every second, caught the prostrate girl by the arm and threw her behind him toward the open door. "Run for your life!" he said.

But she didn't run. She couldn't run, and while she was struggling to get upon her feet, the fellow recovered himself and emitted a roar that acted on her terrified soul as if it had been a blow. She fell incontinently upon her back in a dead swoon.

Mr. Dootleby's situation was perilous. He had hoped by a sudden and overwhelming attack to stun the man and get the girl out into the street. But the man's quick recovery and the girl's exhaustion left him in almost as bad a situation as ever, and he glanced apprehensively at the party upon the benches.

They had scarcely stirred! One of the men, indeed, had risen, and was standing with his hands in his pockets and something in the nature of an amused smile upon his face. The others had so far shifted their positions as to be the better able to see whatever went on, and only one of them manifested the slightest desire to take a hand in the proceedings. This was the little girl of twelve or fourteen. She was intensely excited, and in the moment's pause that succeeded Mr. Dootleby's onslaught she dashed across the room, and lifting the head of the unconscious girl, rested it on her knee, and stroked it soothingly.

"Good for you, my child!" said Mr. Dootleby. "Try to bring her to."

The hideous old scoundrel, as he now turned again to confront Mr. Dootleby, was more hideous than ever. Blood from the wound in his head was trickling over his face, into which the fury of a legion of devils was concentrated. "Sissy!" he bellowed, "go back to yer bench!"

"Don't do it, my child," said Mr. Dootleby. "You're all right. Run outside if it gets too dangerous for you in here."

The fellow gathered himself together, evidently intending to dash past Mr. Dootleby toward the bar beyond. But Mr. Dootleby lifted the poker ominously. "Stand back!" he cried.

A slight chuckle came from the man who had risen from the bench. "Dey don't seem ter be no flies on dis party, Pete!" he said, with a broad grin.

Pete's answer was a scowl and an oath.

"W'y doncher come on, an' help me do him up?" he snorted.

"Wot ud be de use? I t'ink he kin get away wid you, Pete, an' I wanter see de fun. He's chain lightnin', ole man, an' you better be sure of yer holt."

"I'll give all dere is on him if you'll help, Dick!" said Pete.

Mr. Dootleby took his watch, his gold pencil, and a dollar or so in change from his pockets, and tossed them toward Dick.

"That's all I've got," he said. "Now, let us alone."

Dick slid the coins in his pocket and carefully examined the gold watch. "Dere's a good 'eal er sportin' blood in de old gen'l'man, Pete; a good 'eal er sportin' blood," he remarked, with the utmost cheerfulness. "Bein' a sportin' man myself I ainter goin' back on a frien'."

"You're goin' back on your word fast enough!" said Pete bitterly.

"No, I aint. I toljer I wouldn't bodder you. I didn't guarantee nobody else. You sed she was yourn, and you was goin' to make her promise to quit young Swiggsy. I offered to match you five dollars agin de gurl, an' I said if you was to win I wouldn't trouble you. You said if I winned I could have her. All right. I lost, an' I give up my good money. Den you went ter work wallopin' de gurl. You'd er kilt her if dis covey hadn't er lit in. All right, dat wasn't no fault er mine. An' fur all me, he kin stick dat blazin' iron clear down yer t'roat, an' I'll set yere an' take it in widout winkin'."

Mr. Dootleby listened intently to this speech. It afforded him an inkling of the situation.

"Is this girl your daughter?" he said.

Pete was in no humor to parley. He could only growl and swear. When he had relieved himself without, enlightening Mr. Dootleby, Dick spoke again.

"She ain't nobody's darter, ole gent, but he sez she's his gurl. She been keepin' comp'ny wid young Swiggsy, an' she wont promise not ter. Dat's de whole biznuss. De harder he walloped, de more she wouldn't promise."

Mr. Dootleby felt in his arms the strength of a whole army corps. "Look here," he said to Dick, "will you promise me fair play?"

"Dey wont nobody interfere widjer," Dick replied. "I'll be de empire, an' I t'ink I kin referee a mill 'long er de bes'. Sail right in, ole gent. The gurl stan's fer de di'mun' belt. If you knocks out yer man, she's yourn. If he licks you, an' has any strength left, he kin go on wid his wallopin'."

"Sissy's" soothing hand and the fresh air coming through the door had brought back life into the girl's limp body. She was still weak and prostrate, lying at full length on the floor, with her head supported upon Sissy's shoulder.

She was a brilliant type of the ignorant and vicious population which overflows the tenements in certain downtown districts and furnishes the largest element in the city's criminal society. Her eyes were large, and must have been, under better conditions, full of light and expression.

Even now, when great lumps, dark and burning with inflammation, stood out upon her forehead, and heavy sashes of black circled her eyes, while all the rest of her face was white and bloodless and cruelly distorted with pain— even now there was a kind of beauty about her that gave her rank above the class to which conditions, more forceful than laws, condemned her.

Condemned? Yes, condemned; why not? What did she know of the science of morals, of souls, or revelations, or higher laws? Who had ever mentioned these things to her. What had she to do with questions of right and wrong? What was right to her but gratification, or wrong but want? What was passion but nature pent up, or crime but congested nature suddenly set free?

She spoke a Christian tongue. She wore a Christian dress. Her heart answered to the same emotions that quicken or deaden the beat of other breasts. She had tears to shed, hopes to excite, passions to burn, desires to gratify. Nature had denied her none of the faculties that give beauty, and grace and dignity and sweetness to another. Even as she lay stretched on the floor of a dive in the heart of a Christian city, but remoter from influences that encourage the good and repress the bad in her nature than if she were standing in the darkest jungle of Africa—even there, degraded, ignorant, and infinitely wretched, she was a martyr to the very virtues, truth and constancy, of which she knew the least!

Some such reflections as these were flitting through Mr. Dootleby's mind as he glanced down upon her, and then turned to his enraged antagonist, who was standing ever alert for a chance to recover his victim.

"Look here," said Mr. Dootleby. "Let's come to terms about this affair. You can see for yourself that the girl is half dead. You don't want to kill her outright, I'm sure."

"'Tain't no biznuss of yourn if I do," the old man savagely replied.

"Maybe not. But cool off, now, and be reasonable. You'll be sorry enough for what you've done already, and if you were to do more you'd have to stand your trial for murder."

"'Twont be for murderin' her w'en I gits in de jug. But I'll murder you if yer don't leave dis place right off."

"I'm not going to leave till I take her with me."

"Den you wont never leave alive."

Pete whipped a knife from his pocket and rushed at Mr. Dootleby, intending to overwhelm him by a sudden and furious attack. The ivory cane again came into action. It struck the muscular part of Pete's arm just below the shoulder. The knife did not reach its destination, but it inflicted an ugly wound in Mr. Dootleby's hand. Without noticing this, he closed in on his foe, pouring all the resources of his powerful frame into a dozen fierce and well-directed blows. The spectators upon the benches, however indifferent while the brute had been maltreating a defenseless girl, were now seized with a panic. Two of the men slunk out into the street. The girls rushed to their rooms, threw on their coats and street dresses, and escaped also. The battle continued for several minutes, each man fighting, as he knew, for his life.

Pete was a great human beast. He was far stronger than Mr. Dootleby, but not nearly so quick and dexterous. The blow on his right arm placed him at a great disadvantage. Mr. Dootleby knew he could not fight long. Every second drew heavily upon his vitality. But he made no useless expenditure of his strength. His blows were intelligently directed toward the accomplishment of a specific object in the disabling of his enemy, and each of them did its appointed work. At last exposing himself by a sudden lunge, Pete was thrown, and he did not rise. He was unconscious.

So was Mr. Dootleby—almost. His head swam and he leaned heavily against the wall for support. The blood was dripping from several ugly wounds, but he revived as he heard Dick remark: "Dat was a beauterful mill. All right. Bein' a sportin' man myself, I t'ink I knows a good mill w'en I sees one. De di'mun' belt, ole man, is yourn. All right. Hello! W'y, where's de trophy gone?"

Mr. Dootleby opened his one available eye, and saw that the only persons in the room were himself, his beaten enemy, and Dick.

"What's this mean?" he cried. "You pledged your word on fair dealings."

Dick called on all the saints to witness that he did not know where the girl had gone. "De whole crowd cleared out," he said, "w'en de hustlin' begun. But she can'ter gone fur. I reckon if you go out in de street you'll fin' her and de kid wot's helpin' her around somewheres. I'll sponge off Pete, an' try ter patch up wot's lef' of him. All right."

Mr. Dootleby was not slow to act upon this suggestion. He bent over the still prostrate Pete and tried to ascertain if his pulse was beating. It not being immediately apparent whether it was or not, and Mr. Dootleby not caring about it a great deal anyhow, he caught up his hat and coat and hurried away.

Sissy was watching for him from behind a tree across the street, and she came toward him running.

"Maggie's in de alley, sir, yonder by de lamp, layin' dere an' moanin', an' I t'ink dey's sumpin' wrong wid her," said Sissy.

She led him to the spot beyond which they had not been able to escape, where Maggie was lying with the light from the street lamp shining full in her face. Her dress was torn at the neck, for she had not been costumed as the others were, and the cold, wintry night-air was blowing on her bare throat and breast. Her big eyes had lost their dimness, and were blazing with a fire kindled by a wild imagination. Mr. Dootleby took off his hat and knelt upon the alley stones, and threw his arms around her shoulders, supporting her. She looked through him at some one not present but beyond.

"I didn't do it, Swiggsy, an' he couldn't 'a' made me if he'd burned my eyes out like he said he was goin' to!" she whispered faintly. "But he used me rough, Swiggsy, an' I'm—just—a little—bit—tired."

"Good God in Heaven!" murmured Mr. Dootleby, "look upon this wavering soul in Thy full compassion. She is tired, so very, very tired."

"And, Swiggsy, let's go somewheres where he can't fin' me, cause I'm fearful of him. An' you'll get steady work, Swiggsy, tendin' bar, an' then—"

She closed her eyes, and for several moments lay silent and still.

"Swiggsy—"

The sound was faint now, and Mr. Dootleby bent low to catch it.

"I suspicion something ails me in my side, an' I'm falling, falling, falling—— Ketch me, Swiggsy, hold me—I'm honest wid you, don't you know it. Tell me so, and say it loud, so's I can hear. I'll be good to you when I get—rested."

STARS OF THE NIGHT, ARE YOU WATCHING HERE?

The street is empty. Not a sound is heard. Not a footfall. Not a voice. The world is sleeping, dreaming of its own ambitions. Stars of the night, are you watching here?

"You said you t'ought I was pretty, Swiggsy, an' it made me so glad an' happy, 'cause I wants you to think I'm pretty—ah! where are you going! Come back! come back! come back! Don't leave me all alone, please, please don't, for I'm falling again, fast, faster all the time, an' I'll soon fall—"

She opened her eyes wide—wider than ever. She looked into Mr. Dootleby's face and smiled. She lifted her hand and dropped it heavily into his. Her head dropped on his shoulder. She had fallen—out of human sight!

V.

THE HON. DOYLE O'MEAGHER.

At this particular moment the Hon. Doyle O'Meagher is a busy man. Tammany Hall's nominating convention is shortly to be held, and Mr. O'Meagher is putting the finishing touches upon the ticket which he has decided that the convention shall adopt. The ticket, written down upon a sheet of paper, is before him, together with a bottle of whisky and a case of cigars, and the finishing touches consist of little pencil-marks placed opposite the candidates' names, indicating that they have visited Mr. O'Meagher and have duly paid over their several campaign assessments—a preliminary formality which Mr. O'Meagher enforces with strict impartiality. The amount of each assessment depends entirely upon Mr. O'Meagher's sense of the fitness of things. To dispute Mr. O'Meagher's sense in this particular is looked upon as treason and rebellion. In the case of the Hon. Thraxton Wimples, the intended candidate for the Supreme Court, the assessment is $20,000.

Mr. Wimples is a little man of profound learning and ancient lineage. Mr. O'Meagher is a man of indifferent learning and no lineage to speak of. Mr. Wimples's grandfather had signed the Declaration of Independence, and had moved on three separate occasions that the Continental Congress do now adjourn, while no reason whatever existed, other than the one most obvious but least apt to occur to any one, for supposing that Mr. O'Meagher had ever had a grandfather at all. And yet, as Mr. Wimples, though on the threshold of great dignity and power, walks into Mr. O'Meagher's presence, he find himself all of a tremble, and glows and chills chase each other up and down his spinal column.

"Ah, Mr. O'Meagher," he says, "good-morning! Good-morning! Happy to see you so—er—well. Charming day, so warm for the—er—season."

"Yes," says Mr. O'Meagher, "so it be."

"I received your notification of the high—er—honor, you propose to confer on me."

"Yes," says Mr. O'Meagher, "you're the man for the place."

"So kind of you to—er—say so. You mentioned that the—er—assessment was—"

"Twenty thousand dollars," says Mr. O'Meagher, with great promptness.

"JUST SO," SAYS MR. WIMPLES, "JUST SO."

"Just so," says Mr. Wimples, "just so."

"And you've called to pay it," says Mr. O'Meagher, taking up his list and his pencil. "I've been expecting you."

"Ah, yes, to be sure, of course. I was going to propose a—er—settlement."

"A what?" says Mr. O'Meagher sharply.

Mr. Wimples mops his brow. "The fact is," he says, "I don't happen to have so considerable a sum as $20,000 at the—er—moment, and I was thinking of suggesting that I just pay you, say, $10,000 down, and give you two—er—notes."

"'Twont do," says Mr. O'Meagher, shaking his head and fetching his pencil down upon the table with a smart tap, "'twont do at all."

"Eh? Indorsed, you know, by—"

"Mr. Wimples, that $20,000 in hard cash must be in my hands by six o'clock to-night, or your name goes off the ticket."

"O—er—Lud!" says Mr. Wimples, sadly.

"By six P. M."

"But, my dear Mr. O'Meagher—"

"Or your name goes off the ticket."

Mr. Wimples groaned, grasped the whisky bottle, poured out a copious draught, tossed it down his throat, bowed meekly, and withdrew. In the vestibule he met the Hon. Perfidius Ruse, the Mayor of the city, whose term of office was about to expire, and as to whose renomination there was going on a heated controversy. Mr. Ruse was a reformer. It was as a reformer that he had been elected two years before. At that time Mr. O'Meagher found himself menaced by a strange peril. It had been alleged by jealous enemies that he was corrupt, and they called loudly for reform. At first, Mr. O'Meagher experienced some difficulty in understanding what was meant by corrupt and what by reform. His mission in life, as he understood it, was to name the individuals who should hold the city's offices and to control their official acts in the interest of Tammany Hall, and he had great difficulty in comprehending how it could be anybody's business that he had grown rich performing his mission. But perceiving that a large and dangerous class of voters was clamoring for a reformer, he concluded to humor it if he could find a good safe reformer on whom he could rely. In this emergency he had produced the Hon. Perfidius Ruse.

It cannot be said that Mr. O'Meagher regarded the Ruse experiment as entirely satisfactory. Mr. Ruse had certainly reformed several things, and with considerable adroitness and skill, but there were many who said that his reforms had all been made with an eye single to the glory of the Hon. Perfidius Ruse, and with a view to the establishment of a personal influence hostile to the man who made him. The time had now come for the test of strength. Concerning his ultimate intentions, the Hon. Doyle O'Meagher was cold, silent, and reserved.

"How are you, Mr. Mayor?" said the crestfallen Mr. Wimples, as he came upon the reformer in the vestibule. "Going up to see the—er—Boss?"

"I was thinking of it, yes. How's he feeling?"

"Ugly. He's in a dev'lish uncompromising—er—humor. If you were going to ask anything of him I advise you to—er, not."

"Thank you. I only intend to suggest some matters in the interest of reform."

"I wish you well. But—er—go slow."

Mr. O'Meagher did not rise to greet his distinguished visitor. He simply drew a chair close to his own, poured out a glass of whisky, and said, "Hello!"

"I thought I'd just drop in, Mr. O'Meagher," said the Mayor, "to say a word or two about the situation. What are the probabilities?"

"As regards which?"

"H'm, well, the nominations?"

"WHO CAN TELL?" EJACULATED MR. O'MEAGHER.

"Who can tell," ejaculated Mr. O'Meagher. "Who can tell? What is more uncertain, Mr. Ruse, than the action of a nominating convention?"

"To be sure," responded Mr. Ruse. "What, indeed?" Whereupon each statesman looked at the other out of the corners of his eyes.

"There's only one thing I care about," continued Mr. Ruse, "and that is reform. If my successor is a reformer, I shall be satisfied."

"Make yourself easy," replied Mr. O'Meagher. "He'll be a reformer. I've been paying some attention during the last two years to the education of our people in the matter of reform. My success has been flattering. I think I can truthfully say now that Tammany Hall has a reformer ready for every salary paid by the city, and that there's no danger of our stock of reformers giving out as long as the salaries last."

Mr. Ruse hesitated a moment, as if reflecting how he should take these observations. Finally he laughed in a feeble way and said, "Good, yes, very." Then he added, "But, speaking seriously, I do feel that my duty to the public requires me to exert all the influence I have for the protection of reform."

"I feel the same way," said Mr. O'Meagher, "exactly the same way. I'm just boiling over with enthusiasm for reform."

"Then our sympathies and desires are common. Now, if I could feel sure that I ought to run again in the interest of reform—"

"You've done so much already," Mr. O'Meagher hastily put in, "you've sacrificed so heavily that I don't think it would be fair to ask it of you."

"N-no," said the Mayor, dubiously, "I suppose it wouldn't, now, would it?"

"Of course not."

"And yet I don't like to run away from the call, so to speak, of duty."

"Don't be worried about that."

"But I am worried, O'Meagher. I can't help it. By every mail I am receiving hundreds of letters from the best citizens of New-York, urging me to let my name be used. Deputations wait on me constantly with the same request, and, as you know, they are going to hold a mass-meeting to-morrow night, and they threaten to nominate me, whether or no. What can I do? I tell them I don't want to run, that my private business has already suffered by neglect, but they answer imploring me not to desert the cause of reform just when it needs me most. It is very embarrassing."

"Very," said Mr. O'Meagher. "It's astonishing how thoughtless people are. But they wouldn't be so hard on you if they knew how you were fixed."

"That's just it. They don't know, and I don't want to appear selfish."

Mr. O'Meagher coughed, not because he needed to cough, but for want of something better to do.

"The Tammany ticket," Mr. Ruse continued, "will be hotly opposed this year, and I'm bound to say that I don't think it is sufficiently identified with reform. They tell me you are going to nominate Wimples for the Supreme Court. Wimples is a good lawyer, but he has no reform record. Neither has Colonel Bellows, whom you talk of for District-Attorney. McBoodle for Sheriff does not appeal to reformers. Bierbocker for Register might get the German vote, but how could reformers support a common butcher? I don't know whom you think of for my place, but it seems to me that there's only one way to save your ticket from defeat and that is to indorse the candidate for Mayor presented by the citizens' mass-meeting to-morrow night. That would make success certain. The public would praise your noble fidelity to reform, and you'd sweep the city! Think of it, Mr. O'Meagher! What a glorious, what a golden opportunity!"

"My eyes are as wide open as the next man's for golden opportunities, Mr. Ruse," replied Mr. O'Meagher. "But the question is, who will be nominated."

"Well, 'hem! of course I can't definitely say. I'm trying to get them to take some new man. But if they should insist on nominating me, I'm afraid I'd have to—h'm, what—what do you think I'd have to do?"

"Well, being a pious man and a reformer, I should think you'd at least have to pray over it."

The Hon. Perfidius Ruse gave a keen, quick glance at the Hon. Doyle O'Meagher, and slightly frowned.

"I should certainly consider it with care," he said stiffly.

"So should I."

"Is that all you will say?"

"No, I'll say more," and he picked up the sheet of paper on which he had written the names of the Tammany candidates. "Look here," he continued. "This is my list of nominees. The space for the head of the ticket is still blank. I have not told any one whom I mean to present for the Mayoralty, but I will promise you now to insert there the name of the man nominated by your Citizens' meeting to-morrow night."

"Whoever he may be?"

"Whoever he may be."

"And I may rely on that?"

"I SHOULD CERTAINLY CONSIDER IT WITH CARE," HE SAID STIFFLY.

"Did I ever tell you anything you couldn't rely on?"

"No."

"All right. Good-by."

They shook hands, and Mr. Ruse departed wearing an expansive smile. As he left the room, Mr. O'Meagher smiled also and picked up his pen. "I may as well fill in the name now," he said softly, "and save time," and with great precision he proceeded to write: "For Mayor, the Hon. Doyle O'Meagher. Assessed in the sum of—" but there he stopped. "We'll consider that later," he said.

The personal history of the Hon. Doyle O'Meagher strikingly proves how slight an influence is exerted in this young republic by social prestige and vulgar wealth, and how inevitably certain are the rewards of virtue, industry, and ability. I am credibly told that Mr. O'Meagher first opened his eyes in a little ten by twelve earth cabin in the County Kerry, Ireland, though I can not profess to have seen the cabin. Being from his earliest youth of a reflective disposition, he became impressed, when but a small lad, with the conviction that thirteen people, three pigs, seven chickens, and five ducks formed too numerous a population for a cabin of those dimensions. In the silent watches of the night, with his head on a duck and a pig on his stomach, he had frequently revolved this idea in his young but apt mind, and at last, though not in any spirit of petulance, he formed the resolution which gave shape and purpose to his later career.

He had communicated to his father his peculiar views about the crowded condition of the cabin.

"Begob, Doyley, me bye," the old man had replied, "Oi've bin thinkin' o' that. Whin the ould sow litters, Doyley, it's sore perplexhed we'll be fer shlapin' room. Divil a wan o' me knows how fer to sarcumvint the throuble widout we takes you, Doyley, an' the young pigs, an' shtrings ye all up o' nights ferninst the wall."

Doyle waited developments with a heavy heart, and when they came and he found that it required all the fingers on both his hands wherewith to calculate their number, he took down his hat, dashed the unbidden tear from his eyes, and made the best of his way to Queenstown.

The opportunity is not here afforded for an extended review of the stages of progress by which Mr. O'Meagher, having landed in New York, finally secured almost a sovereign influence in its municipal affairs, and yet they are too interesting to justify their entire omission. He first won a place in the hearts of the American people by discovering to them his wonderful fistic attainments. From small and unnoted rings, he steadily and grandly rose until the newspapers overflowed with the details of his battles with the eminent Mr. Muldoon, with Four-Fingered Jake, with the Canarsie Bantam, with Billy the Beat, and with other equally distinguished gentlemen of equally portentous titles, and at last none was to be found capable of withstanding the onslaught of the aroused Mr. O'Meagher. When he went forth in dress-array, belts and buckles and chains and plates of gold armored him from head to heel, and diamonds as large as pigeons' eggs blazed resplendently from every available nook and corner all over his muscular expanse.

Mr. O'Meagher's retirement from the ring was rendered inevitable by the fact that no one would enter it with him, and he found himself compelled to employ his talents in other fields of labor. Reduced to this extremity, he resolved to go into politics, and as an earnest of this intention he fitted up a new and gorgeous saloon. It was a novelty in its way, with its tiled floors, its decorated walls, its costly and beautiful paintings, its rare tapestries, its statues in bronze and marble, its heavy, oaken bar, and its pyramid of the finest cut glass—and when he threw it open to the public he celebrated the occasion by formally accepting a Tammany nomination for Congress.

In the halls of the National Legislature, Mr. O'Meagher soon let it be known that he cared not who made the country's laws, so long as a fair proportion of his constituents were supplied with places and pensions, and his aggressive and successful championship of this principle soon won for him a proud position in the councils of his party. He was a friend of the common people, and the commoner the people the friendlier he was, until, having clearly established his claims to leadership, in obedience to the summons of his organization, he gave himself up to the management of its destinies.

It was as the Boss of Tammany Hall that Mr. Doyle O'Meagher's genius attained its largest and highest development. Notwithstanding the opposition of rival factions engaged in bitter competition with Tammany, Mr. O'Meagher contrived to let out the offices at larger commission rates than Tammany had ever received before. Under no previous Boss had Tammany's heelers enjoyed such vast opportunities for "business." It was all in vain that envious and less-gifted bosses sought to undermine and depose him. Steadily and courageously he pursued his policy of reducing the labor of self-government to individual citizens until he had placed their taxes at a maximum and their trouble at a minimum. They had but to pay, Mr. O'Meagher did all the piping and all the dancing too.

He was in capital humor now as he dropped the pen with which he had written his own name as that of the Mayoralty candidate for whom he had finally decided to throw his important influence, and when a boy entered with the information that Major Tuff was below, the Hon. Doyle O'Meagher was actually whistling.

"Tuff," he said. "Good, I'm wanting Tuff. Send Tuff up."

Tuff entered. Tuff's hat was new and high and shiny. Tuff's hair was all aglow with bear's grease. Tuff's eyes were small and snappy. Tuff's nose was flat and wide and snubby. Tuff's cheeks were big and bony. Tuff's cigar was long and black. Tuff's lips were thick and extensive. Tuff's neck was huge and short. Tuff's coat was a heavy blue one that did for an overcoat, too. Tuff wore diamonds as big as his knuckles. Tuff's scarf was red. Tuff's waistcoat was yellow, and every color known to the spectroscope was employed to make up Tuff's copious trousers.

"Well," said Tuff, "I'm on deck."

"Thank you, Major. How are things looking?"

"Dey couldn't be better. I got t'irty-six tenement houses wid at leas' two hundred woters to de house. Dey's two t'ousan' Eyetalians, five hunered niggers, more'n a t'ousan' Poles, and de res' is all kinds. An' every dern one of em's eddicated!"

"Educated! Really, you don't mean it?"

"WELL," SAID TUFF, "I'M ON DECK."

"Eddicated! You kin betcher boots. De performin' dogs in the circus aint a patch to dem free and intelligent Amerikin citerzens. I got 'em trained so dat at de menshun of de word 'reform' dey all busts out in one gran' roar er ent'oosiasm. I had eight hunered of 'em a-practisin' in de assembly rooms over Paddy Coogan's saloon las' night. I tole 'em de louder dey yelled when I said de word 'reform' de more beer dey'd get w'en de lectur was done. Some of 'em was disposed ter stick out for de beer fust, an' said dey could do deir bes' shoutin' w'en dey was loaded. But my princerple is work fust, den go ter de cashier. So I made 'em a speech.

"I sez: 'Feller-citerzens: Dis is de lan' er de free an' de home er de brav,' an' den I give a motion wot means 'stamp de feet.' Dey all stamped like dey was clog-dancers. Den I cleared me t'roat an' perceeded: 'Dis is de haven of de oppressed, de pore an' de unforchernit from all shores.' I give de signal wot means cheers, an' dey yelled for two minits. 'Dis is our berloved Ameriky!' sez I, 'where no tyrant's heel is ever knowed,' sez I, 'where all men is ekal,' sez I, 'an' where we, feller-citerzens, un'er de gallorious banner of REFORM—' an' at dat word, dey all jes' got up on deir feet an' stamped, an' yelled, an' waved deir hats an' coats till you'd er t'ought dey was a Legislatur' of lunatics. Oh, I got 'em in good shape—doncher bodder about me."

"Ahem," said Mr. O'Meagher thoughtfully, as he cracked his finger-joints and puffed on his cigar. "You've done well, Tuff, excellent. Ah, Tuff, there's going to be a meeting in the Cooper Union to-morrow night. The people that are getting it up—er, well, I'm afraid they're not very friendly to me, Tuff. The doors open at seven. Now, do you think the proceedings would be interesting enough to your friends for them to attend in such numbers as will fill the hall, Tuff?"

"Say no more, Mr. O'Meagher, dey'll be dere."

"In large numbers, Tuff?"

"Dey'll jam de hall."

"Early, Tuff?"

"By half-past six."

"Good. I think you'll find the policemen on duty there very good fellows. You might see me to-morrow morning, Tuff, and I'll have something for you."

VI.

THE HON. DOYLE O'MEAGHER.

(CONCLUDED.)

All bedecked with light and all ablaze with color, the Cooper Union was fast filling up with the friends of Reform. So enormous had the crowds in Astor Place become that, although the hour was early, Colonel Sneekins had wisely concluded to wait no longer, but at once to let them in. They poured through the wide doorways in abundant streams, while Colonel Sneekins led the superb brass band of the 7th Regiment, done up in startling uniforms and carrying along with it a tremendous battery of horns and drums, to its place in the gallery.

Colonel Machiavelli Sneekins sustained an important relation to the Reform movement, and at this Grand Rally of Non-Partisan Citizens in the Interest of Reform, he had, with great propriety, selected himself to be Master of Ceremonies. Colonel Sneekins was a non-partisan citizen. He looked upon partisanship as the curse of the Republic, and in his more enthusiastic moments had declared that if he could have his way about it, any man so hopelessly dead to the nobler impulses of the human heart as to confess himself a partisan should be declared guilty of a felony and confined for a proper period of years at hard labor. What the country called for, according to Colonel Sneekins, was Reform. The first step in bringing about the triumph of Reform was to put all the offices in the hands of Reformers. If the public wished to intoxicate its eyes with the spectacle of the kind of men who would then administer the Government, it had but to look upon him. He was a Reformer. As a Reformer he was in possession of a lucrative municipal office, wherein he was mightily prospering, and which for the honor and glory of Reform he was willing to retain.

Colonel Sneekins was the leading spirit of this citizens' movement. He had prepared the call of the meeting. He had obtained the 1500 signatures now appended to it, representing estimable business men who, in observing that useful maxim of trade, "We strive to please," esteemed it one of their functions to sign all the petitions that came along. Colonel Sneekins had hired the hall and the band; had made up from the City Directory a formidable list of Vice-Presidents and Secretaries; had secured the orators, and finally had arranged for the attendance of a sufficient audience. In perfecting these details he had had the valuable assistance of other distinguished Reformers and non-partisan citizens. Editor Hacker, of *The New York Daily Sting*, had boomed the movement with great zeal and effectiveness. General Divvy, the ex-Governor of South Carolina, who had grown wealthy reforming that State and had thereafter naturally come to be regarded as an authority on all matters connected with reform, had written an earnest letter commending the rally as one of the most important steps that had ever been taken in the direction of pure and frugal government. The Rev. Dr. Lillipad Froth, from his pulpit in the Memorial Church of the Sacred Vanities, had taken occasion to say that great results to the community might be expected from the success of this patriotic enterprise, and ex-Congressman Van Shyster, being interviewed by a reporter of *The Sting*, after expressing his unqualified opinion that all political parties were utterly corrupt and abandoned, whereof his opportunity of judging had certainly been excellent, since he had suffered numerous defeats as the candidate of each of them successively, emphatically declared that he saw no hope for the city except in the cause this meeting was called to foster.

No definite purpose had been expressed in the published call as to what should be done at the Rally, but Colonel Sneekins's plans were fully matured. The Hon. Doyle O'Meagher, the Boss of Tammany Hall, had promised that his organization should indorse for the office of Mayor the nominee presented by the Reformers. As to the identity of their candidate there was but one mind among the Reformers. Who should he be but that champion of Reform, the Hon. Perfidius Ruse? Mr. Ruse was not an experiment. He had already served as the City's Chief Magistrate, and had filled many remunerative offices with Reformers. Being of a modest and retiring disposition, he was now holding aloof from the honors sought to be thrust upon him. He had begged his friends to take some new candidate, he had pleaded his well-known dislike of office and the pressing demands of his private affairs. But, nevertheless, zealous as he was in the Reform cause, he had consented to furnish a delegation of 500 citizens from his morocco factories in Hoboken to swell the Grand Rally in the Cooper Union, and had given his friend, Colonel Sneekins, an ample check wherewith to procure portraits and pamphlets presenting to the public the features and the services of the Hon. Perfidius Ruse. It was Colonel Sneekins's intention totally to disregard Mr. Ruse's plea for rest from official cares, and as he now from behind the wings contemplated the great crowd that was surging into the Cooper Union, he rubbed his hands and gleamed his teeth with such intensity of emotion that the Rev. Dr. Lillipad Froth, who was standing near by, felt his flesh a-creeping.

It was certainly an extraordinary crowd. It had assembled almost in an instant. Scarcely had the policemen taken their places at the doors of the Cooper Union when a bulky, variegated young man stepped up to one of them.

"Hello!" he said.

"Hello, Meejor," responded the officer.

"When'll yer open de door?"

"Air ye wantin' t' git in, Meejor?"

"Doncher know I got a gang to-night?"

"So ye have, Meejor, so ye have. Oi was hearin' about it, av coorse. It's the Tim Tuff Assowseashun, aint it?"

"Now, looker yere!" said Tuff sharply, "Aincher got no orders 'bout dis meetin'?"

"Oi have that, Meejor. Oi was towld that you an' some friends av yourn moight be a-wantin' seats, an' Oi was ter see that ye got 'em."

HE RUBBED HIS HANDS AND GLEAMED HIS TEETH.

"Dat's all right, den. Me an' my frien's 'll be along in about ten minutes, an' dey'll be enough of us ter fill de hall, an' dere's one t'ing yer wants ter keep in yer head, and dat's dis—ef me an' my frien's don't get a chance ter jam dis house before anybody else is 'lowed inside de door, de Hon'able Doyle O'Meagher 'll be wantin' ter know de reason why!"

Having thus delivered himself Tuff sauntered down the Bowery, and presently from all points of the compass a tremendous rabble began to pour into Astor Place and to mass itself in front of the Cooper Union. Tuff himself reappeared in a few moments, and when Colonel Sneekins gave the signal for the doors to be opened Tuff and his friends took easy and complete possession of the house.

Meanwhile the Hon. Perfidius Ruse stood in a little room at the rear of the stage receiving the invited guests of the occasion. Mr. Pickles, the well-known Broome Street grocer, assumed a look of intense morality and importance, as the Mayor asked him how he did and expressed his gratification at seeing the honored name of Pickles—a power in the commercial world—enrolled among the friends of reform. The appearance of General Divvy put the Mayor in quite a flutter, and when the General told him that he positively must consent to run again, and that he was the only hope of the Reformers, the Mayor was much affected.

"I fear I am," he replied, with a mournful shake of the head, as much as to say what a commentary that was on the absence of virtue in public life.

Editor Hacker was equally earnest in his appeals. He said the Mayor must come right out, and referred to a conversation he had had with the President only last week, in which the President had confidentially said he was as much in favor of Reform as ever. Dr. Punk, who stands at the very head of the medical profession, informed the Rev. Lillipad Froth that it was his deliberate opinion, should Mr. Ruse desert them in this crisis, all would be over. Something like dismay was created by the ominous remark of ex-Congressman Van Shyster that others might do as they pleased, but as for him, his mind was made up. At this critical juncture the Hon. Erastus Spiggott, the orator of the evening, opportunely arrived, and upon being told that Mr. Ruse was still hesitating, he boldly declared that the only thing to do was to take the bull by the horns. Fired by the cheers elicited by this observation, he proceeded to say that the occasion which had brought together the large and representative body of citizens assembled in the hall beyond, and waiting only for the opportunity to indorse the wise and safe and honorable administration of Mayor Ruse (loud cheers) and to place him again in nomination, would live in history. (Cries of "good! good!") That vast and intelligent audience was not there to record the edict of corrupt and selfish bosses, but as thoughtful, independent, and patriotic citizens, free from the shackles of partisanship (loud applause), they had come together to promote the honor and the prosperity of this imperial metropolis.

Mr. Spiggott was entirely satisfied that among them there was no division of sentiment as to the course that should be pursued to secure this noble end. They knew as well as he, as well as any of the gentlemen about him now, that the Reform cause stood in peril of but one misfortune—the retirement of the great, unselfish, popular, and devoted man who had already led the Reformers to victory. (Rapturous applause.) He did not fail to appreciate the modesty that led Mr. Ruse to undervalue his magnificent services to the city.

He could well understand his (Mr. Ruse's) desire to return to his counting-room and his fireside free of the burdens and anxieties incident to a great trust. But—and here Mr. Spiggott's bosom swelled and his eyes flashed with a noble fire—he was not here to-night to consider Mr. Ruse's feelings and wishes; he was here, as they all were, in the discharge of a public duty. (Cheers.) That duty required of Mr. Ruse an act of self-sacrifice. He must accept the nomination. He could not, he would not dare desert the Banner of Reform. (Cheers.)

Mr. Spiggott paused, wiped his brow and his eyeglasses, and continued. He might say in this small and select company of Reformers what it might be imprudent to assert later in the evening, when he came to address the great assembly in the outer hall, that the outcome of this meeting was being keenly watched by the spoilsmen. They were a cunning and sagacious lot. The one thing they most dreaded was the very thing this meeting was going to do. He had the best reasons for knowing that Boss O'Meagher mightily desired to nominate a candidate of his own at the Tammany Hall convention. Who had been selected by this unprincipled partisan, this arrogant and odious dictator (loud and long applause), he did not know. But he was certain to be a partisan, a spoilsman, a tool of Tammany Hall and its corrupt boss. Mr. Ruse's nomination to-night would deal a deadly blow to that plot. Tammany Hall would not dare risk the defeat of its entire ticket by nominating a candidate against the Hon. Perfidius Ruse. (Immense enthusiasm.) Indeed, Mr. Spiggott had reason to believe that Boss O'Meagher, cunning trickster that he was, would seek to avail himself of Mr Ruse's popularity and would indorse the nominee of this meeting. Under these circumstances it was folly to think of permitting Mr. Ruse to retire. (Cheers.) It could not be done.

"OF THIS IMPERIAL METROPOLIS."

Mr. Ruse was deeply affected by these remarks, and at their conclusion he touched his handkerchief to his eyes and said he did not think it would be right for him to resist any longer. Thereupon Colonel Sneekins, in a tone of voice that highly distressed the nerves of the Rev. Lillipad Froth, cried out "Hurrah!" and forthwith led the way from the little dressing-room in which they were assembled out upon the stage.

The Reformers had been so busy bolstering up the shrinking nature of Mr. Ruse that they had given small heed to the enormous concourse of citizens in the hall. Indeed, Colonel Sneekins, having ascertained that it would be sufficient in point of numbers for the purposes of a "grand rally," had not bestowed a further thought upon it, so that when he and his vice-presidents and his distinguished guests finally got upon the stage and began to look about them, the spectacle that met their eyes was as unexpected as it was bewildering. From the reporters' tables to the remotest recesses of the gallery the hall was packed tight with a motley mob, in which the element of born cut-throats largely predominated. It was the kind of crowd that could only have been gathered from the three-cent lodging-houses in Chatham Street. A dense volume of tobacco smoke, produced from pipes and demoralized cigar-stumps, choked the room. The evening being rather warm, all surplus clothing had been disposed of, and so far as could be observed through the hazy atmosphere, the audience was attired only in shirts. In one sense it was a highly representative audience. It represented every nation and every clime on the face of the earth. Had it been selected for the purpose of showing the cosmopolitan character of the population in the tenement-house district surrounding Chatham Square, it could not have been more picturesque. Bristle-bearded Russians and Poles, heavy-bearded Italians, dark-visaged Hungarians, and every other manner of unwashed man had been drawn into this Grand Rally of Non-Partisan Citizens in the Interest of Reform.

Colonel Sneekins looked aghast at General Divvy, and whispered hoarsely, "There's been a mistake!" Drawing Mr. Spiggott, Editor Hacker, and ex-Congressman Van Shyster about them, a hurried consultation took place. It was quickly decided that retreat was now impossible and that the meeting must go on. They were assisted in coming to this conclusion by the chorus of lively and altogether friendly apostrophes that came from the audience in cries of "Wot's de matter wid Reform? Oh, it's all right!"

"Let's go right ahead," said Editor Hacker. "This is a democracy, and it is not for us to assume that even the humblest citizen lacks lofty aspirations."

Colonel Sneekins thereupon advanced to the footlights, and was greatly reassured by the hearty applause which his appearance evoked.

"Gentlemen!" he said, and immediately a storm of cheers arose, delaying for several minutes his further utterance. "It affords me pleasure to propose as your chairman to-night the Hon. Cockles V. Divvy."

THE HON. COCKLES V. DIVVY.

General Divvy came forward, and as he bowed and smiled in answer to the wild welcome he received, the band played a few bars from "Captain Jinks." When quiet had been restored, the General said that this was the proudest moment of his life. He should not venture, however, to make a speech. The occasion was one that called for a power of eloquence he could never hope to attain. (Cheers.) He would, however, advert for one brief moment (more cheers) to the significance of this great assembly. He was rejoiced to see so representative a gathering of intelligent citizens, drawn from every walk of life, brought here to consider how best to fix and establish upon the government of the city the great principle of Reform!

The roar of applause that greeted this declaration was simply deafening. For full five minutes the audience cheered and shouted, while Sneekins opened his lips and gleamed his teeth with such vigor as to compel the Rev. Dr. Lillipad Froth to take a more distant chair.

General Divvy called upon Editor Hacker to read the resolutions, which Mr. Hacker, having procured them from Mr. Ruse a moment before, at once proceeded to do. The first resolution, being a declaration in favor of Reform, was instantly carried. The second, which indorsed Major Ruse's administration, was likewise put through with entire unanimity. The third declared that this meeting of non-partisan citizens, anxious to continue to the city the unexampled prosperity it had enjoyed for the past two years, hereby placed in nomination for a second term the Hon. Perfidius Ruse; whereupon, to the horror and dismay of the Reformers, from all parts of the hall came a deafening roar of protesting "noes!"

EDITOR HACKER READS THE RESOLUTIONS.

In an instant confusion and uproar possessed the house. General Divvy pounded the desk before him frantically and screamed for order until he was black in the face. Above all the din arose the shrill shout of Colonel Sneekins, as he called upon the police to clear the room. In the body of the house men were shaking their fists and waving their hats and coats, and calling, "O'Meagher! O'Meagher! 'Rah fer O'Meagher!" So unbounded was their enthusiasm for O'Meagher, so unanimous and determined were they to listen to nothing but O'Meagher, and so fierce and bloodthirsty did their devotion to O'Meagher appear to make them, that General Divvy, warned by the sudden contact of a projected cabbage with his mallet, ceased at once to hammer and picked up his hat and coat. The Reformers about him accepted this as the signal of retreat, and they fled precipitately through the door at the rear of the stage. Of them all only four tarried in the wings, Ruse, Sneekins, Divvy, and Hacker; and as they grasped each other's hands in sorrow and sympathy, they saw the stalwart figure of Major Tuff mount the stage. Immediately the hall was quiet.

"Gents!" said Tuff. "Fer reasons dat I don't see an' derefore can't explain, our leaders 'pear ter hev deserted us and ter hev left dis gran' rally of non-partisan citizens in de int'rust of Reform (cheers) in de lurch. Dis is werry unforchernit, but we, as Reformers, must hump ourselves ter meet de crisis. I nomernate fer Mayor of New York de Hon. Doyle O'Meagher! Long may he wave!"

A cyclone of cheers swept the hall, and as it echoed and re-echoed around them, the four stranded Reformers betook themselves away. "O'Meagher said he would accept the nominee of this meeting as the candidate of Tammany Hall," said Mr. Ruse sadly, "and I guess he'll keep his word."

VII.

MR. GALLIVANT.

Bright and gay was the smile of Mr. Juniper Gallivant. Merry and artless was the flash of his bright blue eyes. Brisk and chipper was the step at which his dainty feet bore him along Broadway. Warm and impulsive was the grasp of his hand.

Mr. Gallivant was a young man, surely not over forty. He was a little fellow with just the slightest perceptible tendency toward stoutness. He could say more words in a minute than any other man in New York, and he, at least, always believed what he said.

Most men, I suppose, believe in themselves, and largely for the reason that most men are but superficially acquainted with themselves. But Mr. Gallivant had been on terms of long and ardent intimacy with himself, and the implicit trust he placed in his own words was therefore as surprising as it was beautiful.

Mr. Gallivant was born a gentleman and educated a lawyer. He had an office in the Equitable Building, and, during his periods of ill-luck, a large and paying clientage. For it was only when luck was against him that he consented to practice at his profession. When it was known that he was in distressed circumstances, clients flocked to him in large numbers. Other less eloquent attorneys retained him to try their cases for them. He had business in plenty.

But when fortune favored him, Mr. Gallivant didn't bother with musty old law books. Not much. He spent all his time spending his money. He had the most novel and ingenious ideas on the subject of loafing. He loafed scientifically, and with great enthusiasm. He put his soul into it, and when Mr. Gallivant's soul got into anything it straightway began to hum. Mr. Gallivant's soul was in many respects similar to a Corliss engine.

Just now, Mr. Gallivant was in very poor circumstances—a condition of things all the more hardly felt because it succeeded, and succeeded suddenly, upon a period of bewildering prosperity. Early in the year 1888 it was observed that Mr. Gallivant's dark red mustaches were curling away at the ends with a lightness and vivacity that they only displayed when things were going well. The quality of the curl in the ends of his mustaches invariably indicated to his friends the state of the market. They could tell exactly whether stocks were up or down and how much so. The sensitive rhododendron is not more surely responsive to the temperature of its environment than was the curl in Mr. Gallivant's mustaches to the tale of the ticker.

In no other way, mark you, did he reveal his interest in the Street and its doings. By not a single quaver was the cheeriness of his snatchy, racy, merry voice affected. By not the fraction of an inch nor a second was his gay little trot altered. But when the ends of his mustache stood out straight, his friends, no matter how slight was their acquaintance with financial matters, knew they were safe in concluding that the country was going to the dogs, while, on the other hand, when those same mustaches finished off in a sprightly little twist, the fact that we were living under a wise and beneficent dispensation was too clear for argument.

Early in 1888, as I said before, Mr. Gallivant's mustaches began to curl. They became elastic. They twisted themselves this way and that in graceful good-humor. They twined themselves lovingly about his nose and danced in constant ecstasy. Mr. Gallivant's office in the Equitable Building saw less and less of him. He left his lodgings in Harlem and took a suite of large and beautiful apartments in a fashionable hotel. Every afternoon he drove a pair of superb black horses over the Boulevard and through the Park. All his friends were happy. They asked and it was given them. He lavished diamond buttons and scarf-pins among them as if he were a prince and they were pugilists. He got up a party and made a palace-car excursion to the Yellowstone Park. He purchased a stock-farm in California. He hired a steam yacht and cruised in the Baltic. From the middle of March until the end of September he used the world as if it were his.

But then, a change came o'er the spirit of his red mustaches. They ceased to sport about his nose. They were distinctly less playful than they had been, and by degrees they became positively stiff. In the mean time, Mr. Gallivant had returned to his law office. He had also gone back to live in Harlem, and one night last December he shut himself in his room—a hall bed-chamber on the third floor, rear—sat himself upon the only chair at hand, stretched his legs in front of him, thrust his hands in his pockets, and murmured:

"I feel curiously like writing an essay on the 'Vanity of Human Wishes'!

"Let me see, let me see," he continued in a ruminating tone, "what's to be done?"

"LET ME SEE—WHAT'S TO BE DONE?"

He ran his hands through his pockets and produced a handful of change. Inspired by this success he rose and went to the closet and continued his search through a choice collection of coats, waistcoats, and trowsers that hung upon its hooks. "Nine dollars and seventy-six cents!" he said, when he had counted the proceeds of his investigation. "Well, I've had a great variety of ups and downs in my short but checkered career, but I never thought the sum total of my cash assets would be expressed in nine dollars and seventy-six cents! After all, life is but an insubstantial pageant, so I think I'll take a pony of brandy and go to bed."

The next day Mr. Gallivant was at his office bright and early. His face shone with its perennial radiance, but his mustache told a cheerless tale. Mr. Gallivant had a number of principles. That which led all the rest was his steadfast refusal to borrow money. He sat down to the contemplation of ways and means, therefore, without the usual recourse taken by impecunious gentlemen with a large circle of wealthy acquaintances to relieve temporary embarrassments. He drew his check-book from his desk and made a careful calculation. "There's the judgment and costs in the Gauber case," he said, "the interest of Robbins's mortgage, the $3000 paid to settle Riker *vs.* Buckmaster, and the money Hunt paid my client Frabsley. Deduct these from my balance in bank, and I have left of my own money the munificent sum of $2.17. There's no way out of it—I must draw on Thwicket!"

It must be owned that in the privacy of his office this conclusion brought something very like a frown upon Mr. Gallivant's brow. "It'll ruin me!" he said. "It'll show Thwicket that I'm as dry as Mother Hubbard's pantry, and when a man loses credit with his broker he might as well shut up shop. But, gad! there's no other way. I must have that balance, positively must, can't wait an hour longer. I've got $380 with Thwicket—$380, all that remains of—well never mind, there's no use grumbling over what's gone. I had a royal good time while it lasted, so I'll just think of the good time and not of what it took to get it. But that $380! H'm, I'll step down and see Thwicket!"

Mr. Gallivant slid into his overcoat, prinked up his scarlet tie, and walked breezily into Wall Street. He chanced to meet Thwicket on the street, and they greeted each other effusively.

"Where under the sun have you been for the last month or so?" exclaimed the broker. "I haven't seen a thing of you."

"Oh, I've been around," answered Mr. Gallivant, with a general wave of the hand.

Mr. Thwicket's face assumed a reproachful look.

"Oh, no," said Gallivant, responsively, "I haven't been doing business with anybody else. Fact is, old fellow, I think I've got a bit flustered. I don't seem able to get the hang of the market. Gad, I've lost a whole fortune since September—must have lost every dollar of a hundred thousand. Now I can't go on like that forever, you know. I give you my word of honor I couldn't stand another such loss. It would put me in a hole."

"Nonsense!" said Thwicket; "come, walk down to the office and we'll talk it over. By the way, where are you living now? I dropped in at your hotel and they said you'd given up your rooms and gone into the country. Queer time o' year to go to the country?"

"Um—well, dunno 'bout that. Found my rooms stuffy. Like country, sleighing, skating, ice yachting, don't you know. Fine air, healthy. Think I'll buy a place up the Hudson. Fact is, negotiating now."

"Really? How's your stock farm?"

"Oh, sold it long 'go. Got tired of it. Can't play with one toy forever, you know. How's the market?"

"It looks to me a little queer to-day," replied the broker.

"That's it! That's what I say. That's the reason I haven't been in lately. Found I was getting rattled. More I figured, further away I got from real conditions."

"It's time to try again."

"H'm; not so sure."

"Luck must change."

"Think so?"

"Oh, I'm certain."

"How's Hollyoke Central selling?"

"It closed yesterday at 86-3/4."

"Good time to buy."

"I doubt that, Mr. Gallivant. It seems to be slowly going the wrong way for buying. But you might sell to advantage."

"There, now, that shows you. I tell you I'm rattled. You see, the very first thing I suggest you discourage. Think I'd better hold off."

They had now reached the broker's office, in which Mr. Gallivant was presently ensconced at ease.

"You are right," said Thwicket, handing out a case of cigars, "in saying that the market is queer. Something very curious has got hold of it. As you know, I avoid giving advice to my customers, and I'm not going to advise you; but if you will notice the state of affairs with regard to Snapshot Consolidated, you will see something that ought to make you open your eyes."

"What is it?"

"Didn't you read the market reports in this morning's papers?"

"Haven't looked at a market report for three weeks."

"I guess that explains why you don't understand the situation, then. Well, Snapshot Consolidated opened at 42. At about noon it began to mount, and it rose peg by peg till it closed at 57-1/2. Now, what do you think of that?"

"I think it's a warning for discreet men like me to keep away from Snapshot. I have no overweening desire to monkey with Mr. Gould, Thwicket." Mr. Gallivant jingled the remnant of six or seven dollars in his pocket and softly added, "He has more money than I."

"You're your own best judge, of course. But if that stock opens this morning above the point at which it closed last night, there's going to be more fun to-day in Wall Street than we've had for many a year. It looks to me like a rock-ribbed corner."

Mr. Juniper Gallivant bowed his head as if in deep reflection. As a matter of fact, he was fermenting with excitement. He looked at his watch. It was within fifteen minutes of the time for the Exchange to open. "A corner!" he softly exclaimed to himself. "A corner, ye gods! and my balance in the Chemical Bank is $2.17. A corner, and I not in it!"

Mr. Gallivant's fingers began to itch viciously, and the perspiration broke out copiously under his thick red hair. By a great struggle he managed to suppress all outward signs of his emotion, while he continued to commune with his own mind. "It's no use," he thought. "I must give up all idea of laying in with a corner when I haven't got money enough to set up a decent champagne supper. No, I must draw that $380, and the question is, how to do it and keep my credit good. Ha! an idea strikes me!" He turned quietly to the broker and said aloud: "Give me a pen, Thwicket!"

He took a blank check from his pocket-book—a check on the Chemical Bank, wherein $2.17 reposed peacefully to his credit.

"I don't think you have very much money of mine here, Thwicket?" he continued, as he slowly wrote the date-line in the check.

"Don't think we have. Robert, what is Mr. Gallivant's balance?"

The clerk turned over his ledger and presently replied: "Mr. Gallivant has a credit of $382.22."

"ROBERT, WHAT IS MR. GALLIVANT'S BALANCE?"

"I don't think we'll bother with Snapshot Consolidated, Thwicket. Truth is, I'm afraid of it. My wits haven't been working right here lately. But I'll just give you a check for $20,000, and you can buy me a nice little block of Michigan Border—say a hundred shares, just to see how the cat jumps, you know."

Thwicket took the check, but with a troubled air. "My dear Gallivant," he said, "why do a thing like that? I'm very glad to have another order from you, but I don't want to see a valuable customer like you lose any more money. Michigan Border was doing very well a month ago, but it is declining now, and for good reasons. Let's take a flyer in Snapshot!"

"Hand me that check!" said Mr. Gallivant in a most decisive tone and with a profoundly irritated air. "Hand it back, Thwicket! Hand it right over, and draw me a check for my balance of $382.22. I'm going to cut the d—d Gordian knot and get out of this! No use talking, my head's all bemuddled. 'F I was to go into the Street to-day I'd lose my whole fortune. Now, don't argue with me, old man, I'm out of sorts, and the best thing for me to do is to stop right short till I get clear-headed again. Draw me that check. Let me have every penny I've got on your books. I'm going up to my place in the country and spend a month reading Greek plays. If anything 'll calm me, that will."

The broker looked vastly disappointed, but smiled consentingly. He returned the $20,000 check, which Mr. Gallivant tore to pieces with a great show of nervousness and irritation, and in another moment, possessed of his precious $382.22, he departed gloomily.

But a long and cheery smile, that reached nearly to the tips of his mustache and almost sufficed to give them a faint curl, spread itself over his face as he turned from Wall Street into Broadway. He caressed the check with his fingers and softly observed, "H'm, I flatter myself that was well done. I have the money, and Thwicket has an abiding confidence in my wealth,—but oh, ye gods! what would I give to be able to put my fine Italian hand into that Snapshot corner!"

Mr. Gallivant returned to his office and endeavored to fasten his attention upon the records of a title search prepared by his clerk, but he found himself ever going over the figures, 57-1/2, 57-1/2, 57-1/2.

"Heavens!" he said presently, "I can't stand this any longer. I must see the ticker. I must find out how it opened to-day. Gad, I'll go crazy if I sit here all day mumbling '57-1/2!'"

He started up and had half put on his coat, when the office door was flung open and Thwicket rushed in breathless.

"Seventy-two," he shouted wildly. "Opened at sixty-five! Leaped right up to 68, then to 70, then to 72. Now's your chance, old man. Say the word and say it quick. Never mind about the $20,000. We'll settle up when the day is over, and every second you lose now will cost you hundreds of dollars. It's sure to go to 160. Don't keep me waiting—say the word?"

Mr. Gallivant jammed his hands deep into his pockets to prevent their betraying his excitement, and hemmed and hawed.

"Do you really think it's worth while, Thwicket!"

"Great guns, man! You make me—"

"Now, don't be nervous, Thwicket. When I trust a man to spend my money for me I want him cool and calm."

"But you're losing valuable time! It's jumping up every minute. The Exchange has gone wild! Everybody's in a furor. You can make a mint if you go right in."

"All right, drive ahead. But use judgment, Thwicket. Remember I don't want to invest more than $20,000, and you should preserve your equanim—"

"SEVENTY-TWO," HE SHOUTED WILDLY.

But Thwicket was gone, and when the door closed behind him Mr. Gallivant gave a leap from the floor where he stood to the sofa eight feet away! Then he leaped back. Then he picked up a pair of dumb-bells and swung them fiercely at the imminent risk of his head and the furniture of the room. Then finally he drew from his desk a bottle of brandy and took a long, strong pull.

"Ah," he said, smacking his lips, "now I'll get ready and go to the street and watch the tumult."

Disposing, as soon as he could, of the correspondence on his desk, he presently made his way to Thwicket's office. The broker was still at the Stock Exchange. He grabbed at the tapes and looked for Snapshot. There was nothing on them but Snapshot. "Snap. Col. 93," "Snap. Col. 96-3/8," "Snap. Col."—even as he stood by the ticker and watched the machine roll out its stream of white paper—"Snap. Col. 108!"

Mr. Gallivant's eyes blurred. He felt queer in his knees. The perspiration broke out fiercely all over his plump little body. "Why the mischief doesn't Thwicket come in?" he murmured. "Why don't he sell and get out of this? Ten, twenty, thirty—great guns! I've made $50,000 already! It can't go on like this much longer. It'll break in half an hour, 'gad, I know it will—I feel it in my bones! If Thwicket doesn't sell inside of thirty minutes I'm a goner, and what's worse, he'll be a goner with me! What's this! 117! By the great horn spoon, I must get hold of Thwicket! Thwicket! Thwicket! My kingdom for Thwicket!"

Mr. Gallivant dropped the tapes and rushed frantically into the street and across to the entrance of the Exchange. He dispatched a messenger across the floor to find his broker, but who could find which in that tumultuous mob? The Exchange floor was crowded with a crazy body of yelling men, their faces boiled into crimson, their eyes glowing with a fierce fire, their hats banged out of shape, their coats in many cases torn into shreds, jostling, tumbling, jumping, stretching all over each other in riotous confusion. Fat men were being squeezed into pancakes, little men were being covered out of sight, tall men were being clambered upon as if their manifest destiny were to serve as poles, and every man of them, big, short, thin, fat, lank, and heavy, was flourishing his arms in the air and howling at the top of his voice!

Mr. Gallivant's messenger returned in a few moments with the report that Mr. Thwicket could not be found. Quivering with excitement, Mr. Gallivant started forth in further search. At the door of the Exchange he met his office-boy, who told him the broker was searching for him high and low—had been at the office and was now in the Savarin café. Thither Mr. Gallivant rushed as fast as his legs could carry him, only to learn that Thwicket had just gone out asking every man he met if he had seen Gallivant. The lawyer was in despair. He glanced at the ticker—"Snap. Col. 134-1/2!"

"Heavens!" he shrieked, "will nobody seize that crazy Thwicket and hold him till I come!"

He ran at full speed to the broker's office. Thwicket had left two minutes before, having learned that Gallivant was at the Savarin. He turned around again and started once more to dash forth, when he saw the broker coming along in reckless haste.

In an instant Mr. Gallivant was all repose—all serenity and ease. He dropped quietly into a chair and picked up the morning paper. In rushed Thwicket, disheveled, frantic, breathless.

"At last!" he cried. "It's 136. It'll break in another ten minutes! Hadn't I better get from under?"

"Still excited, Thwicket?" answered Mr. Gallivant reproachfully. "My dear boy, I'm afraid you've not got a proper hold upon yourself. Yes, probably you'd better unload. Perhaps now's as good a moment as any. But be—"

"YOU'VE DONE VERY WELL, THWICKET."

Thwicket did not wait for the rest. He fled. When he returned half an hour later his face was radiant, but his collar wilted. "Sold!" he cried, "at 148, and busted at 152!"

By a quick, spontaneous motion, Mr. Gallivant's mustaches drew themselves in a loving curl around his nose, but for the rest he was merely cheery—gently cheery—as he always was.

"You've done very well, Thwicket," he said commendingly. "You've quite justified my confidence. You're a knowing fellow, and I'll—er—what's the proceeds?"

"A hundred and thirteen thousand—rather a fair day's work."

"That it is. Send around your check for the hundred, and let the thirteen stay on account. By-by, I'll see you again in a day or two."

Mr. Gallivant walked out into the street upon his usual ramble. "Strikes me," he said musingly, "that I ought to do something handsome for Thwicket now—I really ought. My profit is $113,000. I doubt if his will reach even $500. That doesn't look quite fair, seeing that he did the business all on his own money. The deuce of it is, though, that it's demoralizing to make presents to your brokers. After all, business is business!"

VIII.

TULITZ.

With the circumstances that brought Tulitz into trouble we have nothing to do. Indeed, whatever I may have known about them once I have long ago forgotten. I seem to remember, but very vaguely, that he stabbed somebody, though, at the same time, I find in my memory an impression that he forged somebody's name. This I distinctly recall, that the amount of bail in which he was held was $5000—a circumstance strongly confirmatory of the notion that his assault was upon life and not upon property. In this excellent country, where property rights are guarded with great zeal and care, and the surplus population is large, we charge more for the liberty of forgers than of murderers. Had Tulitz committed forgery, his bail bond would scarcely have been less than $10,000. Since, beyond all question, it was only $5000, I think I must be right in the idea that he stabbed a man.

It was in default of that sum, $5000, that Tulitz, commonly called the Baron Tulitz, alias d'Ercevenne, commonly called the Marquis d'Ercevenne, was committed to the Tombs Prison to await the action of the Grand Jury. At this time Tulitz—I call him Tulitz without intending any partiality for that name over the alias of d'Ercevenne, but merely because Tulitz is a shorter word to write. I doubt if he had any preference between them himself, except in the way of business. He was just as likely, other things being equal, to present his card bearing the words "M. le Marquis d'Ercevenne," as his other card with the words upon it "Freiherr von Tulitz." It has been remarked frequently that when he was the Baron his tone and manner were exceedingly French, while when he was the Marquis he spoke with a distinct German accent. None of his acquaintances was able to account for this.

But as I was saying, when Tulitz was sent to the Tombs he was in hard luck. Formerly he had whipped the social trout-stream with great success. As the Marquis he had composed some pretty odes, had led the German at Mrs. de Folly's assembly, had driven to Hempstead with the Coaching Club, and had been seen in Mrs. Castor's box at the opera. As the Baron Tulitz, he had attended the races, and had been a frequenter of all the great gaming resorts. The newspapers called him a "plunger," and a story went the rounds, in which he was represented to have wrecked a pool-seller, who thereupon committed suicide. The Baron always denied this story, which the Marquis often repeated. Indeed the Marquis was often quoted to the Baron as an authority for it.

But the tide had turned, and now Tulitz was on his back with never a friend to help him. "Fi' t'ousan' tollaire!" he exclaimed, as the Justice fixed his bail, blending both his French and his German accent with strict impartiality, "V'y you not make him den, dwenty, a huntret t'ousandt!"

A penniless prisoner in the Tombs is not an object of much consideration, as Tulitz discovered to his profound disgust. For two days he paced his cell with the restless, incessant tread of a caged hyena. He disdainfully rejected the beef soup, the hunk of bread and the black coffee served to him more or less frequently, and for two days and nights he neither ate nor spoke. The Tombs cells are built of thick stone, entered through a heavy iron door, that is provided with a small grating. Tulitz's cell was on the second tier. Around this tier extends a narrow gallery, along which the guard walks every now and then, to see that all is as it should be. The guard annoyed Tulitz. Every time he passed he would peer in and give a sort of grunt. This became painfully exasperating to the Baron.

"FI' TOUSANT TOLLAIRE! VY YOU NOT MAKE HIM A HUNTRET TOUSANT?"

Late in the afternoon of the second day of his imprisonment, Tulitz, desperate with hunger, rage, and despair, sat down upon the stool in his cell and glared viciously at the grating. The guard's face was there.

"Ha!" cried Tulitz, in a shrill voice, "keep avay! You tink I von tam mouse, and you ze cat, hey? You sit outside ze cage viz your claw out and your tail stiff, ready to pounce on ze mouse. *Mon Dieu!* How I hate!"

The guard unlocked the iron door and stepped inside. "Don't make sech a racket over nawthin'," he said. "De warden says yer gotter do some eatin'."

"I kill ze warden if he keep not his *mechant chute!*"

"Wotcher goin' ter do? Starve?"

"If I choose starve, how you prevent him, hey? How make you me eat? *Voilà, bête!*" Tulitz drew himself to his full height, turned up his shirt-sleeves and bared his great, muscular arm.

"Oh, all right," said the guard. "It's all one to me. Starve if yer wanter. I'm agreeable."

"I vant notting, *rien, rien!*" said Tulitz. "I vant to be leave alone."

"Dat aint much. Mos' people wat comes here is more graspin'. Mos' people wants ter git out."

"Ha!" said Tulitz.

"De warden said fer me ter come in here an' tell yer' he'd send fer anybody yer wanter see."

"Zere is nopotty."

"Aincher got no friends?"

"Ven I haf money, I have friend—*beaucoup,* more friend as I know vat to do viz. I haf no money now."

"Wot's your bail?"

"Fi' tousant tollaire! Bah! Vat is fi' tousant tollaire? Many time I spend him viz no more care as I light my cigar. A bagatelle! But," and he added this with a curiously grim expression, "I haf no bagatelle to-day."

The guard sidled up to Tulitz and whispered in his ear, "What'll yer gimme if I gitcher a bondsman?"

"Ha!" said Tulitz, "you haf ze man?"

"I knows a man," replied the guard reflectively, "who might do it on my recommend. Sometimes, w'en a man aint got no frien's, but kin lay aroun' 'im an' scoop tergedder a couple er hundred dollars, I mention him ter my frien' wid a recommend, an' dat settles it, out he comes."

"Two hundret tollaire!" cried Tulitz, almost piteously. "Ven I efer t'ink my liperty cost me two huntret tollaire and I haf not got him. Zis blow kill all zat is to me of my self-respect! *Je suis hors de moi-même!*"

"Why, you orter be able to raise dat much tin," said the guard.

Tulitz jumped from his bed to the floor with a cry such as a wild beast might have given as it sprang from peril into safety. He demanded pencil and paper, and with them he scribbled a message. "Send for me zat note!" he said. "Bring me a *filet de b[oe]uf*, a *pâte de fois gras*, and a bottle of Burgundy, and bring him all quick! Corinne! *La belle* Corinne! *Chérie amie*, vot I haf svear I lofe and cherish! I haf not remember you, Corinne!"

A throng of people, big and little, young and old, were waiting in the corridors of the warden's office the next morning, eager for the bell to strike the signal that would admit them into the prisons. They were mostly women. Here and there in the crowd was a little boy carrying a tin can with something in it good to eat, sent, doubtless, by his old mother to her scamp of a son. The little beggar has his first experiences of a prison administering to the comforts of his big, ruffianly brother, probably a great hero in his eyes.

For the most part, the crowd is made up of young women. There, muffled closely, is the wife of a defaulter, who was caught in the act. Three days ago she held her head as high as any. Now it is bent low and hidden with shame. Yonder, terrified and broken-hearted, is the sister of a man who shot another. He is no criminal. There was a quarrel about a matter of money. The lie was given, a blow followed, and then a shot. Her brother a murderer! Her brother, all kindness, docility, and goodness, locked up in a place like this with thieves and hardened convicts! It was a fatal shot—ah, me, so very fatal, so widely fatal!

Many of them, though, are laughing and joking with each other. They have got acquainted coming here to look after their husbands, lovers, brothers, fathers, and sons. They bow cheerily as they come in, and say what a fine day it is, and how they missed you yesterday, and they hope nothing was the matter at home. Among them are brazen jades who chatter saucily with the guards, and these are the best treated of all. They are asked no gruff, surly questions, but with a wink and a jest in they go.

On the outer edge of the crowd, among those who waited till the first rush was over, stood a dark, wiry little woman with a face remarkable alike for its resolution and its innocence. She could not have been more than twenty-five years old. She looked as if she had seen much of the world, but had illy learned the lessons of her experience. This combination of strength and simplicity had wrought a curious effect upon her manner. There was no timidity about her, but much gentleness. She was modest and clothed with repose, and yet the outlines of her face plainly informed you that in the presence of a sufficient emergency she was quite prepared to go anywhere or do anything.

"I want to see Monsieur Tulitz," she said to the entry clerk, when her opportunity came.

He gave her a ticket without asking any questions, except the formal ones, and then turned her over to the matron.

The matron of the Tombs has been there many years, and she knows how to read faces.

"Your ticket says you are Madame Tulitz?" said the matron.

"Yes."

"I must search you."

"Very well."

"It must be thorough."

"Very well."

"I WANT TO SEE MONSIEUR TULITZ," SHE SAID.

"Please take off your hat and let down your hair."

She did as she was bidden, and a great mass of dark hair tumbled nearly to her feet. The matron immediately and with practiced dexterity twisted it up again. Then her shoes, dress, and corsets were removed, until the matron was enabled to tell that nothing could by any possibility be concealed about her.

"It's all right," said the matron. "I'm sorry to trouble you so much, but I have to be very careful."

"You needn't apologize. Now can I go?"

"Yes."

She adjusted her hat and proceeded through the long corridors out into the prison yard, and thence into the old prison where Tulitz was confined. The guard who had sent her Tulitz's letter led her to his cell, and brought a stool for her to sit upon outside his grated iron door.

"My *ravissante* Corinne!" cried Tulitz.

She put her fingers through the bars, and he bent to kiss them, coming, as he did so, in contact with two little files of the hardest steel.

"*Diable!*" he said.

"I had them in my hat. I made them serve as the stems of these lilies."

"Ze woman she make ze wily t'ing. How young and *charmante* she seem for one so like ze fox! Ah, Corinne, my sweetest lofe—"

"You don't mean that."

"Not mean him! *Mon Dieu!* How can you haf ze heart to say ze cruel word. Corinne, you are ze only frient I haf in ze whole bad worlt."

"Yes, I know that. But not the only wife."

"Why you torture me so, Corinne?"

"I wont. We'll let it go. You need me, I suppose?"

"You use all ze cold word, Corinne. I neet you! *Oui, oui,* I efer neet you. I neet you ven I stay from you ze longest. I neet you ven ze bad come into my heart and drive out ze good and tender, and leave only ze hard, and make me crazy and full of dream of fortune. Zen I am out of myself and den I neet you ze most, Corinne. Zat I haf been cruel and vicked, I know, but I am punish now. Now, I neet you in my despair, but if you come to speak bitter, I am sorry to haf send for you."

"I'll not be bitter, Tulitz. I don't believe you love me, and I never will believe it again. So don't say tender things. They only make me sad. Tell me what—"

"You do pelief I lofe you."

"No."

"*Chérie.*"

"Don't, Tulitz!"

"You know I haf a so hot blood. It tingle viz lofe for you and I am sane. Zen I dream. I see some strange sight—power, money, ze people at my feet—ze people I hate, bah! I see zem all bend. Zen I am insane and my very lofe make me vorse. Ah, Corinne, if you see my heart, you vould not speak so cold. If I could preak zis iron door zat bar me from you and draw you close to me, Corinne, vere you could feel ze quick beat zat say, 'lofe! lofe! lofe!'— if I could take your hand and kees—"

"Tulitz!"

"My sveetheart!"

"Hush, please, Tulitz. Don't say those things now. I can't stand them. I shall scream. Tulitz, I love you so!"

"Ah, I know zat. You haf no dream zat rob you of your mind. And I shall haf no more soon. Ven ze trial come, and ze shury make me guilty, and ze shudge—"

"No! no! You must escape."

"Ze reech escape, little von. Ze poor nefer. Zat is law. Ha! ha! you know not law. Law is ze science by vich a man who has money do as he tam please and snap his finger—so! and shrug his shoulder—so! and say, 'You not like it? Vat I care, Monsieur?' and by vich ze poor man, vedder he guilty or not, haf no single chance, not von, to escape. I haf not efen ze two huntret tollaire zat gif me my liberty till ze trial come."

"Neither have I, Tulitz, and the only way I can get it is to part with something I love better than—never mind, you shall have the two hundred dollars."

"You mean our ring, Corinne?"

"Yes."

"You shall not sell ze ring. Nefer!"

"But I must. We will get it back."

"No, I forbid! I stay here first." Corinne's face fairly glowed with tenderness.

"Let me do as I think best, darling," she said. "The first thing is to get you out of this wretched place. Now tell me all about it."

He told her all, or, at least, all he needed to tell, and she left him with the understanding that she should meet the guard in the City Hall Park two hours later and arrange about the bail-bond with a man whom he should present to her. She hurried up-town and collected in her lodgings half a dozen valuable pieces of jewelry. These she took to a pawnshop and upon them she realized something more than the sum necessary to obtain Tulitz's bondsman. At the appointed hour she was walking leisurely through the Park, and soon found herself approaching two men. One she recognized as the guard. The other was an elderly man dressed in a black suit of broadcloth which, in its time, had been very fine indeed. But it was made for him when he was younger and less corpulent than now, and he bulged it out in a way that was trying to the stitches and the buttons. His silk hat was shiny, but exceedingly worn, and the boots upon his feet, despite his creditable efforts to make them appear at all possible advantage, were in a rebellious humor, like a glum soldier in need of sleep. His hair was bushy and gray, and his mustache meant to be gray, too, but his habit of chewing the ends of his cigars had resulted in its taking on a yellow border.

"Dis is the gen'l'man wot'll go on Mr. Tulitz's bond, mum," said the guard. "His name's Rivers."

"Madam Tulitz, I am your humble and obedient servant. Colonel Rivers, Colonel Edward Lawrence Rivers, and most happy in this unfortunate emergency to serve you. I have read in the papers of M. Tulitz's disagreeable—er—situation. It is a gross outrage. The bail is $5000, this gentleman tells me. Infamous, perfectly infamous! The idea of requiring such a bond for so trivial an affair. When I was in Congress I introduced an Amendment to the Constitution providing that no bail should be demanded in excess of $500. It didn't get through; the capitalistic influence was too much for me. However, I'd just as lief, to tell the truth, go on M. Tulitz's bond for five thousand as for one. I know he'll be where he's wanted when the time comes, and if he isn't, the bail-bond will. They'll have that to console themselves with, anyway."

"MADAME TULITZ, I AM YOUR HUMBLE AND OBEDIENT SERVANT."

"Where are we to go?" asked Corinne.

"To the police court. I'll show you; but when we get there you mustn't ask me any questions. Ask anybody else but me. I'm always very ignorant in the police court—never know anything, except my answers to the surety examination. Those I always learn by heart. Now—" he turned to the guard, and said parenthetically, "All right, my boy," whereupon the guard disappeared. "Now, just take my arm, if you please; you needn't be afraid, ha! ha! I'm old, and wont hurt you. You see, we must be friends, old friends. Bless you, my child, I've known you from a baby, knew your father before you, dear old boy, and promised him on his dying bed I'd be a father to his— er—by the way, my dear, what's your name?"

"Corinne. Do you want my maiden name?"

"No, never mind that. I always supply a maiden name myself when I deal with ladies, on the ground, you see, that it's much better to keep real names out of bail-bonds, even where they don't signify. In fact, the less real you put in, anyhow, the better. My signature must be on as many as a thousand bail-bonds first and last, in this city, Boston, Chicago, San Francisco, and other places, and I've never yet experienced the slightest trouble. I think my good fortune is almost wholly due to the circumstance that I never repeat myself. I always tell a new story every time."

"Do they know you at the place where we're going?"

"I fervently hope they don't, my dear. It wouldn't do M. Tulitz any good, or me either, if they did. No, no, you must introduce me. I am your friend, your lifelong friend, Colonel Edward Lawrence Rivers. I am a retired merchant. Formerly I dealt in hides—perhaps you had better say in skins, my dear; on second thought, it might be more appropriate to say in skins, and then again it would be more accurate. I like to tell the truth when I can conveniently and without prejudice to the rights of the defendant. If I haven't dealt in skins as much as any other man on the face of the earth, then I don't know what a skin is. Ha! ha! my dear, I think that's pretty good for an old man whose wits are nearly given out with the work that has been imposed upon them. Let me say right here that the clerk of the court is a knowing fellow, and you want to mind your p's and q's. You want to be very confiding and affectionate in your manner toward me, and I'll do all the rest."

"Is there any danger, sir? Will we be found out? Oh dear! I'm dreadfully nervous."

"Well, now, you needn't be, my child, you needn't be. I've had a great deal of experience in delicate matters of this kind, and I guess we'll fetch your husband out all right. As for the danger, it's all mine, and as for getting found out, that will come in due time, probably; but when it comes we'll all of us endeavor to view it from a remote standpoint, where we can do so, I dare say, with comparative equanimity. So keep up your spirits, my dear, and trust to your old friend, the friend of your childhood, Colonel the Hon. Edward Lawrence Rivers, formerly a dealer in skins. Ah, here we are! Just take a look at my necktie, child. Is it tied all right? And is my diamond pin there? No? Well, where the mischief can it be? Ah, yes, here it is in my pocket. My jewel cases are all portable. There! Now, we're ready. Look timid, my child, but confident in the final triumph of your just and righteous cause. Come on."

They entered the court-room. Seated in an inclosure in the custody of an officer was the Baron Tulitz. His sharp face lighted when he saw them approaching, and, as Corinne took her seat by his side, he pressed her hand. Presently his case was called, and his lawyer arose to offer bail. He presented Colonel Rivers. The old man was a spectacle of grave decorum. He answered the questions put to him about his residence, his family, his place of business and his property, which he conveniently located in Staten Island, Niagara County, Jersey City, and Morrisania. He was worth $300,000. He owed nothing. He displayed his deeds. He had never been a bondsman before. He didn't know Tulitz, but was willing to risk the bail to restore peace to the troubled mind of this poor little child, the orphan of his old friend and neighbor. Never was there a bondsman offered more unfamiliar with the forms and ceremonies necessary to the record of the recognizance. He had to be told where he should sign, and even then he started to put his name in the wrong place. But at last it was done, and Tulitz was free.

Corinne's eyes were full of tears when the old man gently drew her arm within his and led her from the court-room, with Tulitz and his lawyer following. He walked with them as far as Broadway, and then he turned to say good-by. He kissed her hand gallantly, and called Tulitz aside.

"Skip!" he said, "and be quick about it!"

IX.

MR. McCAFFERTY.

An incident of the late municipal election has recently come within my knowledge, which I hasten to communicate to the public, in the hope that an investigation will be ordered by the Legislature, and, if the facts be as they are represented here (this being a faithful record of what I have been credibly told), in the further hope that the men who have tampered with the honor of Dennie McCafferty and his friend, The Croak, will speedily be brought to justice.

Late one night toward the close of September Dennie was walking down Houston Street toward the Bowery, when he suddenly espied The Croak walking up Houston Street toward Broadway. As suddenly The Croak espied him, and both stopped short. They looked at one another long and intently, and then Dennie wheeled around and without a word led the way into a saloon near at hand.

"Dice!" said he to the bartender. He rattled the box and threw. "Three fives!" he cried.

DENNIE M'CAFFERTY.

The Croak handled the dice-box with great deliberation. Presently he rolled the ivories out. "Three sixes," he said slowly, "an' I'll take a pony er brandy."

"That settles it!" cried Dennie joyously. "It's you, Croaker, sure pop. My eyes did not deceive me. I thought they had, Croaker. I thought I must be laboring under a mental strain. When I saw you coming up the street I says to myself, 'That's The Croak.' Then I took another look, and says, 'No, it can't be. The Croak's in Joliet doing three years for working the sawdust.' Then I looked again and I says, 'It must be The Croak. There's his cock-eye looking straight at me through the wooden Indian in front of the cigar-store across the street.' Then I looked once more, and says, 'But it can't be. Three years can't have passed since The Croak and I were dealing faro in old McGlory's.' Once again I looked, and I says, 'If it's The Croak, he'll chuck a bigger dice than mine and stick me for drinks, and he'll take a pony of brandy.' There's the dice, there's the pony, and there's The Croak. Drink hearty!"

They lifted their glasses and poured down the liquor, and Dennie continued, "How'd you get out, Croaker?"

"Served me term," said The Croak shortly.

TOZIE MONKS, THE CROAK.

"What! Then is it three years? Well, well, how the snows and the blossoms come and go. We're growing old, Croaker. We're nearing the time when the fleeting show will have flet. And hanged if I can see that we're growing any wiser, or better, or richer—hey? Thirty cents! Ye gods, Croaker, that man says thirty cents! Thirty cents, and my entire capital is a lonely ten-cent piece that I kept for luck. Thirty cents, and my last collateral security hocked and the ticket lost! Croaker, I'm in despair."

The Croak dived into his trowsers pocket, took out a small roll of bills, handed one to the bartender and another—a ten-dollar greenback—to Dennie.

"Dear boy!" said Dennie, expanding into smiles. "What an uncommon comfort you are, Croaker. Virtues such as yours reconcile me to a further struggle with this cold and selfish world. It has used me pretty hard since I saw you last, Croaker. Not long after you left for the—er—West I met an elderly gentleman from Bumville, whom I thought I recognized as a Mr. Huckster. I spoke to him, but found myself in error. He said his name wasn't Huckster, of Bumville, but Bogle, of Bogle's Cross Roads. I apologized, left him, and at the corner whom should I see but Tommy, the Tick. Incidentally I mentioned to Tommy the curious circumstance of my having mistaken Mr. Bogle, of Bogle's Cross Roads, for Mr. Huckster, of Bumville.

"'Bogle!' said Tommy. 'Bogle! Why, I know Bogle well. He's a great friend of my uncle's.' Whereupon Tommy hurried off after Bogle. I am not even yet informed as to what took place between Bogle and Tommy, further than that they struck up a warm and agreeable acquaintance; that they stopped in at a dozen places on their way up-town; that poor old Bogle got drunk and happy; that they went somewhere and took chances in a raffle, and that they got into a dispute over $2000 which Bogle said Tommy had helped to cheat him out of. A couple of Byrnes's malignant minions arrested Tommy, and not satisfied with that act of tyranny and oppression, they actually came to my lonely lodgings and arrested me. What for? you ask in blank amazement. Has an honest and industrious American citizen no rights? Must it ever be that the poor and downtrodden are sacrificed to glut the maw of that ten-fold tyrant at Police Headquarters? They charged me with larceny, with working the confidence game, and despite my protestations and the eloquence of my learned counsel, who cost me my last nickel, a hard-hearted and idiotic jury convicted me, and that sandy-haired old flint at the General Sessions gave me a year and six months in Sing Sing. Now, Croaker, when you live in a land where such outrages are committed upon a man simply because he is poor, you wonder what your fathers fought and bled and died for, don't you, Croaker?"

"I dunno 'bout dat, Dennie, but 'f I cud talk like er you I'd bin an Eyetalian Prince by dis time, wid a title wot ud reach across dis room an' jewels ter match," and The Croak looked at his friend in undisguised admiration.

But Dennie's humor was pensive. "Croaker," said he, drawing the ten-dollar bill out of his pocket and nodding suggestively to the bartender, "look out there in the street. See that banner stretched from house to house. It reads:

'Liberty and Equality! Labor Must Have the Fruits of Labor!' Now what infernal lies those are! There's no liberty here; and as for equality, that cop blinking in here through the window really believes he owns the town. That stuff about labor is all humbug—molasses for flies. They're going to have an election to choose a President shortly. What's an election, Croaker? It's political faro, that's all. The politicians run the bank. Honest fellows, like you and me, run up against it and get taken in. The crowd that does the most cheating gets the pot. Ah, Croaker, what are we coming to?" This thought was too much for Dennie. He threw back his head and solaced himself with brandy.

"As I remarked a moment ago, Croaker," he said, "I have just returned from—er—up the river. You have just returned from—er—the West. Our bosoms are heaving with hopes for the future. We want to earn an honest living. But when we come to think of what there is left for us to do by which we can regain the proud position we once had in the community, we find ourselves enveloped in clouds."

"I was t'inking er sumpin', Dennie," The Croak replied, reflectively, "jess when I caught sight er you. Your speakin' bout polertics makes me t'ink of it some more. W'y not get up a 'sociashun?"

"A what?"

"A 'sociashun. Ev'rybody's workin' de perlitical racket now; w'y not take a hack at it, too?"

"Anything, Croaker, anything to give me an honest penny. But I don't quite catch on."

"Dey's two coveys runnin' fer Alderman over on de Eas' Side. One of 'em's Boozy—you knows Boozy. He keeps a place in de Bowery. De udder's a Dutchman, name er Bockerheisen. Boozy's de County Democracy man, Bockerheisen's de Tammany. Less git up a 'sociashun. You'll be president an' do de talkin.' I'll be treasurer an' hol' de cash."

"Croaker, you may not be eloquent, but you have a genius all your own. I begin dimly to perceive what you are driving at. I must think this over. Meet me here to-morrow at noon."

The district in which the great fight between Boozy and Bockerheisen was to occur was close and doubtful. Great interests were at stake in the election. Colonel Boozy and Mr. Bockerheisen were personal enemies. Their saloons were not far apart as to distance, and each felt that his business, as well as his political future, depended on his success in this campaign. A third candidate, a Republican, was in the field, but small attention was paid to him. A few days after Dennie and The Croak had their chance meeting in Houston

Street, Dennie walked into Colonel Boozy's saloon. Boozy stood by the bar in gorgeous array.

"How are you, Colonel?" said Dennie.

"It's McCafferty!" cried the Colonel, "an' as hearty as ever. As smilin', too, an' ready, I'm hopin', ter take a han' in the fight fer his ould frind."

"I am that, Colonel. How's it going?"

"Shmokin' hot, Dennie, an' divil a wan o' me knows whose end o' the poker is hottest."

COLONEL BOOZY.

"It's your end, Colonel, that generates the heat, and Dutchy's end that does the burning."

"There's poorer wit than yours, Dennie, out of the insane asylums. I'll shtow that away in me mind an' fire it off in the Boord the nexht time I make a speech. If I had your brains, lad, I'd a made more out av 'em than you have."

"You've done well enough with your own," said Dennie. "They tell me it's been a good year for business in the Board, Colonel."

"Not over-good, Dennie. The office aint what it was once. It useter be that ye cud make a nate pile in wan terrum, but now wid the assessmints an' the price of gettin' there, yer lucky if ye come out aven."

"The trouble is that you fool away your money, Colonel. You ought not to hand over to every bummer that comes along. You should be discreet. There's a big floating vote in this district, and you can float still more into it if you go about it the right way."

The Colonel looked curiously into Dennie's ingenuous blue eyes, and said with an indifferent air, "Ye mought be right, and then agin ye moughtn't."

"Oh, certainly, we don't know as much before election as we do after."

"Is yer mind workin', Dennie? Air ye figgerin' at somethin'?"

"Oh, no; I happened to meet The Croak this morning—you know The Croak, he's in the green-goods line?"

"Do I know him? Me name's kep' on his bail-bond as reg'lar as on the parish book."

"Yes, of course; well, I met him, as I was saying, and, to make a long story short, I found that Bockerheisen had got hold of him, and they've packed a lot of tenement-houses with Poles and Italians and organized an association. There are about 600 of them. Dutchy keeps them in beer, and that's about all they want, you know."

Colonel Boozy had been about to drink a glass of beer as Dennie began this communication. He had raised the glass to his lips, but it got no further. His eyes began to bulge and his nose to widen, his forehead to contract and his jaws to close, and when Dennie stopped and drained off his amber glass, the Alderman was standing stiff with stupefied rage. He recovered speech and motion shortly, however, and both came surging upon him in a flood. He fetched his heavy beer-glass down upon the bar with a furious blow, and a volley of oaths such as only a New York Alderman can utter shot forth like slugs from a Gatling gun. When this cyclone of rage had passed away he was left pensive.

Dennie, who had remained cool and sympathetic during the exhibition, now observed: "It is as you say, Colonel, very wicked in Dutchy thus to seek to win by fraud what he never could get on his merits. It is also most ungrateful in The Croak. Well, I've told you what the facts are. You'll know how to manage them. So-long," and Dennie started for the street.

But the Colonel detained him. "Don't be goin' yet, Dennie," he said. "I want ter talk this bizness over wid ye. Come intil the back room, Dennie."

They adjourned into a little private room at the rear of the bar, and the Alderman drew from a closet a bottle of wine, a couple of glasses, and a box of cigars.

"Dennie," he said nervously, "we must bate 'em. That Dootch pookah aint the fool he looks. Things is feelin' shaky, an' you mus' undo yer wits fer me an' set 'em a-warkin'. If the Dootchy kin hev a 'sosheashin, I kin, too. If he kin run in Poles an' Eyetalyans, I kin run in niggers an' Jerseymen."

Dennie contemplated a knot-hole in the floor for several minutes. "No, Colonel," he said, at last, "that wont do. There's a limit to the number of repeaters that can be brought into the district. If we fetch too many, there'll be trouble. Dutchy has put up a job with the police, too, I'm told; they're all training with Tammany now. Besides, if you get up your gang of six or seven hundred, you don't make anything; you only offset his gang. You must buy The Croak; that'll be cheaper and more effective. Then you'll get your association and Dutchy will get nothing. You will be making him pay for your votes."

Boozy grasped Dennie's hand admiringly. "It's a great head ye have, Dennie, wid a power o' brains in it an' a talent fer shpakin' 'em out. I'll l'ave the fixin' av it in your hands. Ye'll see The Croak, Dennie, an' get his figgers, an' harkee, Dennie, if ye air thrue to me, Dennie, ye'll be makin' a fri'nd, d'ye moind!"

While Dennie was thus engaged with Boozy, The Croak was occupied in effecting a similar arrangement with Mr. Bockerheisen. In a few gloomy but well-chosen words, for The Croak, though a mournful, was yet a vigorous, talker, he explained to Bockerheisen that a wicked conspiracy had been entered into by Boozy and McCafferty to bring about his defeat by fraud, and he urged that Mr. Bockerheisen "get on to 'em" without delay.

MR. BOCKERHEISEN.

"Dot I vill!" said the German savagely, "I giv you two huntered tolars for der names of der men vat dot Poozy mitout der law registers!"

"I aint no copper!" cried The Croak, angrily. "Wot you wants ter do is ter get elected, doncher?"

"Vell, how vas I get elected mit wotes vat vas for der udder mans cast, hey?"

"You can't," said The Croak, "dey aint no doubt 'bout dat."

"If dey vas cast for him, dey don't gount for me, hey?"

"No."

"Den I vill yust der bolice got und raise der debbil mit dot Poozy."

"Hol' on!" the Croak replied. "If dey was ter make a mistake about de ballots, an' s'posen 'stead of deir bein' hisn dey happens to be yourn, den if dey're cast fer you dey wont count fer him, will dey?"

Mr. Bockerheisen turned his head around and stared at The Croak in an evidently painful effort to grasp the idea.

"If Boozy t'inks dey're his wotes—"

"Yah," said Bockerheisen reflectively.

"And pays all de heavy 'spences of uniforms an' beer—"

"Yah," said Bockerheisen, with an affable smile.

"But w'en dey comes to wote—"

"Yah," said Bockerheisen, opening his eyes.

"Deir ballots don't hev his tickets in 'em—"

"Yah!" said Bockerheisen quickly.

"But has yourn instead—"

"Yah-ah!" said Bockerheisen, rubbing his hands.

"Den an' in dat case who does dey count fer?"

Mr. Bockerheisen leaned his head upon his hand, which was supported by the bar against which they were standing, slowly closed one eye, and murmured, "Yah-ah-ah."

"I t'ought you'd see de p'int w'en I got it out right," said The Croak.

"How you do somedings like dot?"

"Dat aint fer me to say," The Croak diffidently remarked. "But dey do tell me dat dat McCafferty has a grudge agin Boozy, an if you wants me ter ask him ter drop in yere an hev a talk wid ye, I'll do it."

Mr. Bockerheisen did not fail to express the satisfaction he would have in seeing Mr. McCafferty, and Mr. McCafferty did not fail to give him that happiness. The association sprang quickly into being, and its rolls soon showed a membership of nearly 700 voters. Two copies of the rolls were taken, one for submission to Alderman Boozy and one to Mr. Bockerheisen. This was in the nature of tangible evidence that the association was in actual existence. In further proof of this important fact, the association with banners representing it to be the Michael J. Boozy Campaign Club marched past the saloon of Mr. Bockerheisen every other night, and the next night, avoiding Mr. Bockerheisen's, it was led in gorgeous array past the saloon of Colonel Boozy, labeled the Karl Augustus Bockerheisen Club. As Mr. Bockerheisen looked out and saw Colonel Boozy's association, and realized that whereas Boozy was planting and McCafferty was watering, yet he was to gather the increase, a High German smile would come upon his poetic countenance, and he would bite his finger-nails rapturously. And, on the other hand, as Colonel Boozy heard the drums and fifes of the Bockerheisen Club, and saw its transparency glowing in the street, he would summon all his friends to the bar to take a drink with him. It is said that even before election day, however, the relations between Dennie and the Colonel on the one hand, and between The Croak and Bockerheisen, on the other, became painfully strained. It is said that Boozy was compelled to mortgage two of his houses to support Bockerheisen's club, and that Bockerheisen's wife had to borrow nearly $10,000 from her brother, a rich brewer, before Bockerheisen's wild anxiety to pay the expenses of Boozy's club was satisfied. Dennie acknowledged to the Colonel a couple of days before the election that he had found The Croak a hard man to deal with, and that it had been vastly more expensive to make the arrangement than he had supposed it would be. The Croak's manner, as I have said, was always subdued, if not actually sad, and in the presence of Bockerheisen, as the election drew near, he seemed to be so utterly woe-begone and discouraged that the German told his wife he hadn't the heart to quarrel with him about having let McCafferty cost so much money. Besides, as the Colonel remarked to Mrs. Boozy on the night before election, when she told him he had let that bad man, McCafferty, ruin him entirely, and as Bockerheisen said to Mrs. Bockerheisen when she warned him that that ugly-looking Croak would be calling for her watch and weddingring next—as they both remarked, "What is the difference if I get the votes of the association? Business will be good in the Board of Aldermen next year, and I can make it up."

Who did get the votes of the association I'm sure I can't say. All I know is that the Republican candidate was elected, and a Central Office detective who haunts the Forty-second Street depot reported at Headquarters on Election Day night that he had seen Dennie McCafferty, wearing evening dress and a single glass in his left eye, and Tozie Monks, The Croak, dressed as Dennie's valet, board the six o'clock train for Chicago and the West.

X.

MR. MADDLEDOCK.

Mr. Maddledock did not like to wait, and, least of all, for dinner. Wobbles knew that, and when he heard the soft gong of the clock in the lower hall beat seven times, and reflected that while four guests had been bidden to dinner only three had yet come, Wobbles was agitated. Mrs. Throcton, Mr. Maddledock's sister, and Miss Annie Throcton had arrived and were just coming downstairs from the dressing-room. Mr. Linden was in the parlor with Miss Maddledock, both looking as if all they asked was to be let alone. Mr. Maddledock was in the library walking up and down in a way that Wobbles could but look upon as ominous. Again, and for the fifth time in two minutes, Wobbles made a careful calculation upon his fingers, but to save his unhappy soul he could not bring five persons to tally with six chairs. And in the mean while, Mr. Maddledock's step in the library grew sharper in its sound and quicker in its motion.

There was nothing vulgar about Mr. Maddledock. His tall, erect figure, his gray eyes, his clearly cut, correct features, his low voice, his utter want of passion, and his quiet, resolute habit of bending everything and everybody as it suited him to bend them, told upon people differently. Some said he was handsome and courtly, others insisted that he was sinister-looking and cruel. Which were right I shall not undertake to say. Whether it was a lion or a snake in him that fascinated, it is certainly true that he impressed every one who knew him. In some respects his influence was very singular. He seemed to throw out a strange devitalizing force that acted as well upon inanimate as upon animate things. The new buffet had not been in the dining-room six months before it looked as ancient as the Louis XIV. pier-glass in the upper hall. This subtle influence of Mr. Maddledock had wrought a curious effect upon the whole house. It oxydized the frescoes on the walls. It subdued the varied shades of color that streamed in from the stained-glass windows. It gave a deeper richness to the velvet carpets and mellowed the lace curtains that hung from the parlor casements into a creamy tint.

"IN THE MORGUE," SAID MR. MADDLEDOCK, "WELL, THAT'S THE BEST PLACE FOR HIM."

Mr. Maddledock's figure was faultless. From head to heels he was adjusted with mathematical nicety. Every organ in his shapely body did its work silently, easily, accurately. Silver-gray hair covered his head, falling gracefully away from a parting in the middle of it. It never seemed to grow long, and yet it never looked as if it had been cut. Mr. Maddledock's eyes were his most striking feature. Absolutely unaffected by either glare or shadow, neither dilating nor contracting, they remained ever clear, large, gray, and cold. No mark or line in his face indicated care or any of the burdens that usually depress and trouble men. If such things were felt in his experience their force was spent long before they had contrived to mar his unruffled countenance. Though the house had tumbled before his eyes, by not a single vibration would his complacent voice have been intensified. He never suffered his feelings to escape his control. Occasionally, to be sure, he might curl his lip, or lift his eyebrows, or depress the corners of his mouth. When deeply moved he might go so far as to diffuse a nipping frost around him, but no angry words ever fell from his lips.

Five, seven, ten, fifteen, twenty minutes had passed since the hall clock had sounded the hour and Wobbles's temperature had risen to the degree which borders on apoplexy. What might have happened is dreadful to conjecture had not Dinks, the housekeeper, come to his relief with the sagacious counsel that he wait no longer, but boldly inform Miss Emily that dinner was served.

Wobbles was just on the point of acting upon this advice when the library call rang, and he hurried to respond.

"You said this note was left here by a tall man, didn't you, Wobbles?" said Mr. Maddledock.

"Yezzur," said Wobbles.

"And he said he would call for an answer?"

"Yezzur, at seven be the clock, zur."

"But it's past seven, Wobbles?"

"Yezzur, most 'arf an howr, most 'arf."

"That will do, Wobbles—and yet, stay. Did you ask his name?"

"Yezzur. Hi did, zur, and 'e says, sezee, 'Chops,' sezee, 'you need more salt,' sezee, 'go back to the gridiron,' sezee."

"Well, that's curious," said Mr. Maddledock; "was he sober?"

"'E 'med be in cups, zur, but they be quiet uns."

"Yes—well, if he calls during dinner, Wobbles, you may show him into the office and stay with him, Wobbles, until I come."

"'CHOPS,' SEZEE, 'YOU NEEDS MORE SALT!' SEZEE. 'GO BACK TO THE GRIDIRON,' SEZEE."

"Yezzur, hexackly, zur, I see, zur. Dinner is served, zur, but Mr. Torbert be not come. Shall I tell Miss Emily?"

"Yes, to be sure. How absurd of Torbert! Why, it's quite late. When I go into the parlor, which will be in another minute, Wobbles you may announce dinner."

Wobbles bowed himself away and Mr. Maddledock sat himself down. He picked up the note to which he had just referred, and read it through carefully. Then he rubbed his eyeglass, stroked his nose reflectively, crumpled the note in his hand, and tossed it into the grate fire before him. He rose and stood watching it burn. "Only two things are possible," he said, quietly. "I must shoot him or pay him, and I don't feel entirely certain which I'd better do." Then he walked into the parlor.

"You're almost as bad as Mr. Torbert, father," said Miss Maddledock. "I've been waiting long enough for you, and now we'll all go to dinner."

"Torbert's late, is he?" said Mr. Maddledock, as if this were the first he had heard of it, bowing gravely to the others. "How's that, Linden?"

"I'm sure I can't account for it at all, sir," answered the young man. "We took breakfast together, and at that hour he was in full possession of his faculties. His watch was doing its accustomed duty, and there was no sign of any such condition in or about him as would suggest the possibility of preposterous behavior like this."

"Perhaps his business keeps him," said Miss Maddledock amiably.

"Ho, ho," chuckled Mrs. Throcton, in her jolly way, "if he depended on that to keep him, he'd be ill kept, indeed."

"Why, mamma," said Miss Throcton, reprovingly, "how can you?"

"And why not, Nancy, my child? Bless me! how perfectly absurd to think of Torbert, all jewels and bangs, with a business. I'll leave it to Mr. Linden if he ever earned a penny in his life."

"But that is not the test of having a business, dear Mrs. Throcton," Linden replied. "I know some wonderfully busy men, whose earnings wouldn't keep a pug dog."

"Now more than likely something's the matter with his clothes," remarked plump Miss Nancy, in tones of deep sympathy. "I've often been late because I couldn't get into mine."

"While we speculate the dinner cools," said Miss Maddledock suggestively. "Father, will you give your arm to Mrs. Throcton? Mr. Linden, there stands Miss Nancy. I will go alone and mourn for Mr. Torbert."

"Now, this is really too bad," said Linden, when they were seated at the table. "It is a form of social misconduct which goes right at the bottom of Torbert's character. When he comes I'll tell him the story of a friend of mine who never was late for dinner in his life, and who consequently—"

"Died!" interrupted Mrs. Throcton. "I know he did. Any man who never was late for dinner in his life must in the nature of things have had a short time to live."

"Come to think of it," said Linden, "he did die, and I never suspected why before. He was the last man in the world whom I should have thought the dread angel would want."

"Oh, you never can tell," Mrs. Throcton cheerily declared. "It's all luck, pure luck. This man died because it isn't in fate for any man who is never late to dinner to live long, but still living is all luck. If the 'dread angel,' as you call him, happens to look your way and fancies you, why, off you go—plunk! like a frog in the pond."

Mrs. Throcton had scarcely concluded this genial doctrine before the belated guest, all bows, smiles, and graceful attitudes, was rendering homage to Miss Maddledock.

"Sir!" she said, "you will kindly observe that my aspect is severe. You are indicted for—for—what is he indicted for, Mr. Linden?"

Linden was a lawyer, and he answered promptly: "For violating Section One of the Code of Prandial Procedure, which defines tardiness at dinner as a felony punishable by banishment from all social festivities at the house where offense is given, for a period of not less than two nor more than five years."

"You hear the—the—what are you, Mr. Linden—something horrid, aren't you?"

"He is, or his looks belie him," interjaculated Torbert.

"The prosecutor, your Honor," replied Linden, "prepared, with regard to this prisoner, to be as horrid as I look."

"May it please the Court," began Torbert, with mock gravity, "I find myself the victim of an unfortunate situation, and not a conscious and willing offender against the Prandial Code. Justice is all I ask. More I have no need for. Less I am confident your Honor never fails to render."

"Now, Mr. Prosecutor, where's my judicial temperament gone that you compliment me upon so often?" demanded Miss Maddledock, turning sharply to the lawyer. "I had it a moment ago, together with a frown; where have they gone?"

"They will return directly I call your Honor's attention to the flagrant nature of the prisoner's crime," said Linden—"a crime so utterly atrocious—"

"True, you do well to remind me. Justice you called for, sir. Very well. Justice you shall have. Go on!"

"Your Honor is most gracious. That part of the indictment which charges me with having an engagement to dine with your Honor at seven P. M. is admitted. I left my house in plenty of time, but—"

Mrs. Throcton (*sotto voce*).—Does the prisoner live in Harlem?

Miss Nancy.—Or in Hoboken?

The Court (with great dignity)—If the prisoner is going to put his trust in the saving grace of the elevated cars or the tardy ferry, the Court would prefer not to delay its consommé listening to such trivial excuses. The Court's soup is growing cold.

A roar of laughter greeted this observation, and Mr. Linden remarked, "The prosecutor feels it his duty to suggest that the prisoner enter a plea of guilty, and throw himself at once upon the Court's mercy."

"The distinguished assistants to the prosecutor," said Torbert, turning with an extravagant bow toward Mrs. Throcton and Miss Nancy, "think to throw contempt upon the defense by associating it with Harlem and Hoboken. Let them beware. Let them not tempt me to extremities. There are insults which even my forbearing spirit will not meekly endure. Had they said Hackensack—"

The Court—Well, what then?

"Then, your Honor, I should have objected; and had your Honor ruled against me, I should have been reluctantly compelled to demand an exception! But let me come at once to my defense. My offense, if offense it is, was caused by the necessity which was imposed upon me of unharnessing a man."

"What!"

"Of unharnessing a man, please your Honor! A man coming north and a horse going east endeavored to cross the street at a given point, at one and the same moment. It proved an impossibility, and they—er—intersected."

"Dreadful!" cried Miss Maddledock.

"It so impressed me, else I had not dared to risk your Honor's displeasure by pausing to unharness the man."

Mrs. Throcton, merry soul that she usually was, had grown quite serious when Torbert spoke of a collision and an accident. Her voice was earnest as she said, "Now, Mr. Torbert, stop your jesting right away and tell us what you mean."

"It was as I have said, and all done in a second," Torbert replied. "You never can tell just how a thing like that is done, you know. The horse was a runaway. It must have come some distance, for it had broken away from the vehicle to which it had been attached, and its torn harness was held upon it by only one or two feeble straps. The man was a tall, queer-looking fellow, rather seedily dressed, and possibly not quite sober. He had been walking just ahead of me for several blocks. I can't say what it was about him that first attracted my attention. Possibly it was a peculiarity in his walk."

Mr. Maddledock, who had not spoken a word since they sat down to dinner, now glanced up, and said, in an inquiring tone, "A peculiarity in his walk?"

"Yes," answered Torbert, dropping into his seat and picking up his oyster fork, "and I am somewhat at a loss to describe it. I don't think he was lame, or wooden-legged, or afflicted with any hip trouble. As I recall the step now, it seems to me that it was merely a habit. I think he took a long and then a short step, long and short, long and short."

**"HE WAS AN ODD-LOOKING FELLOW," SAID TORBERT,
"ODD AND BAD."**

"Um," said Mr. Maddledock.

"Just as he approached the crossing where the accident occurred he turned his head, and I don't think I ever saw a more Mephistophelean countenance. The only thing that broke the dark-angel shape of his face was his nose, and that, with slight alterations, would have made an excellent shepherd's crook."

Mr. Maddledock took up his wine-glass and drained it at a single quaff. "A shepherd's crook," he repeated; "an odd nose, truly."

"He was an odd-looking fellow all over," Torbert continued, "odd and bad. I never was more disagreeably impressed with a human face in my life. Well, when we reached the corner we both heard the clatter of the horse's hoofs on the cobbles and looked up. He was coming on at a fearful rate, and people were shouting at him in a way that must have increased his frenzy. Quite a crowd had collected, and this fellow and I were jostled forward upon the crossing. I shouted to the crowd not to push us, and pressed back with all my strength. He was just ahead of me. He had two means of escape—to hold back as I had done, or to dash forward. He hesitated, and that second's pause was fatal. The horse plunged forward, struck him squarely, knocked him heavily upon the stones, and left him there, covered with the remnants of its harness, which having become caught in his coat, somehow or another, were drawn off its back."

THE HORSE PLUNGED FORWARD, STRUCK HIM SQUARELY, AND KNOCKED HIM HEAVILY UPON THE STONES.

"Terrible!" cried Miss Maddledock, "Was he much hurt?"

Mr. Maddledock leaned forward and bent his ear to catch the answer.

"I don't know how much, but certainly enough to make his recovery a matter of doubt."

Mr. Maddledock slightly frowned. "A—matter—of—doubt?" he repeated, pausing with singular emphasis on each word.

"Yes, of grave doubt," answered Torbert, "and dread too, for even if he gets well again, he must be maimed for life, and he was the sort of creature that ought not to have a deformity added to his general ugliness."

Emily Maddledock had been leaning her chin upon her hand with a thoughtful look in her face for several minutes. As Torbert paused, she said: "Your description of that man brings a face to my mind that I saw recently somewhere. I can't seem to remember about it clearly, though the face is very distinct."

"Indeed?" said Torbert. "Now, that's curious. If you've ever seen the beggar you ought to remember it. There's one other mark upon him that may serve to place him still more clearly before you. Directly over his left cheek-bone there is a long rectangular mole—"

"Yes! yes!" cried Emily. "I remember. Why, father—"

Mr. Maddledock had been sipping his wine. As Emily suddenly looked up and addressed him, he twirled the glass carelessly between his thumb and finger, remarking, as if this were the only feature of the story that at all impressed him, "A mole, did you say? What a monstrosity!"

"Um, well, is it?" Torbert replied. "Can't say I'd thought of that."

"Don't think of it!" sharply remarked Mrs. Throcton, as if annoyed at the interruption, "but go on."

"Several of us sprang forward from among the crowd and set at work trying to free him from the confining straps. How in the world they contrived to get around him and to tie him up as they did is a mystery. We cut them loose, lifted him up, and found him quite unconscious. Somebody thoughtfully rang for an ambulance. Before it came we carried him into a drug store close by and the druggist plied him with restoratives. I supposed he was dead, but the drug man said he wasn't. He had shown no sign of life, however, when the ambulance arrived. They took him off, and I, having made myself somewhat more presentable than I was, called a carriage and am here."

Then turning to Miss Maddledock he smilingly continued: "I now move, please your Honor, for the dismissal of the indictment against me on the ground that the evidence does not show any offense to have been committed."

"I think you'll have to grant the motion, Emily, my dear," said Mr. Maddledock, fixing his gray eyes upon his daughter in a way that always riveted hers upon him and drew her mind after them to the complete exclusion of everything except what he intended to say. "Mr. Torbert's defense strikes me as all we could demand. You remarked a moment ago that his description suggested a face to your mind, but you couldn't remember where you saw it."

"I know now," she said. "It was this very afternoon—"

"Exactly," said her father, interrupting rather adroitly than quickly. "It was while we were standing together at the parlor window."

Emily's face flushed, and had any one been looking at her intently he might have had his doubts whether or not that was the time. She did not answer, however, and before any one had begun the conversation anew, Wobbles entered with a card upon his tray which he delivered to Mr. Maddledock.

"Since your Honor is so indulgent," said Mr. Maddledock, as he glanced at the scrawl upon the bit of cardboard and bowed to his daughter, "and with the approval of the prosecutor, I am constrained to ask the Court's consent to a further violation of the Prandial Code. I don't know whether the punishment for leaving the table before the dinner is concluded is greater or less than for a tardy appearance, but I fear I must risk it."

"I suggest, in view of this prisoner's previous good character," said Linden, "that your Honor suspend the sentence."

Mr. Maddledock bowed himself out and walked directly to a little room just off the hall which he used as a private office. A timid young man was waiting for him.

"Well, sir?" said Mr. Maddledock.

"I am an orderly, sir, if you please, at the Bellevue Hospital. A man was brought there, this evening, sir, pretty well done up by a runaway. After he'd been fixed a bit he asked me for his coat, and when I fetched it he took out this bundle of papers and put them under his pillow. The doctors didn't bother him much, for they saw he was a goner, and when he asked if he could live they told him no. He didn't say no more, but when we was alone he asked me to take out the papers from under his pillow. I did it, and he asked me if he died to fetch them here and give them to you in your own hands, and said you'd give me ten dollars for my trouble. So as soon as I was off duty I fetched 'em, and here they are, sir."

"Yes," said Mr. Maddledock, adjusting his eyeglasses and examining them slowly one by one. "Yes. They appear to be all here. Ten dollars, did he say? Well, here it is. Good-night."

"Good-night, sir."

"And the man? Wait a bit. What became of him?"

"Oh, he's dead, sir. The horse done him up. He's dead and in the Morgue by this time. Good-night."

The orderly went out, and Mr. Maddledock stood quietly with the bundle of papers in his hands until he heard the click of the vestibule door. Then he struck a match and fired them one by one, watching each until it was entirely consumed.

"In the Morgue," he said, as the last pale flame flickered and died away. "Well, that's the best place for him. There's no doubt in my mind, not the least, but that that amiable horse saved me from being the central figure in a murder trial. What an odd world it is, to be sure!"

XI.

MR. WRANGLER.

On your way to the Cortlandt Street Ferry, which is on everybody's way to everywhere, and on the left-hand side of the street when you turn out of Broadway, and not very far from the ferry-house itself, there is a little old, low brick building which has stood there a good many years and is going to stand a good many more if Billy Warlock knows himself, and he thinks he does. You may talk about progress all you please, but Billy will soon give you to understand that the only kind of progress which will take that house from him, or him from it, is the progress toward the stars, and that, while he hopes to take it in the Lord's good time, he isn't ready for just yet. Billy Warlock owns that house and lives in it and does business there, and the great big heart that thumps in Billy's great big body and gives strength to Billy's great big arm, loves every individual square inch of brick and earth and planking and plaster in that old house from cellar to scuttle. Part with it! Speculate on it! Sacrifice it to progress! Well, scarcely. Not if you were to offer him its weight in solid gold. Not if its neighbor on one side were a Mills Building and its neighbor on the other an Equitable. Not if you were to build an elevated railroad around it and run ten trains per minute, day and night. So long as Billy Warlock can keep himself above ground, so long will that old house keep him company, and so long will his forges blow fiery sparks in the cellar, while he hammers and hums and hums and hammers on the anvil by his side.

It was just twelve years ago on Christmas Eve that Billy Warlock bought the smithy in the cellar of that little old house. Billy had been working for the man who owned it, and the man who owned it, being a little short of wind and a trifle weak in his legs, had decided to sell and retire. Billy had become the purchaser, and not without many qualms and doubts as to the wisdom of assuming such heavy responsibilities. Billy knew he was a good mechanic, and could put a tire on a wheel or a shoe on a horse as quickly and as well as the next man. But it took a good big pile of dollars, as Billy counted dollars, to get those forges, and before he turned them over to his late employer Billy scratched his head a good many times and did a power of thinking. But at last he let go the dollars, and laid his big fist on the biggest forge and blew a blast through the coals that made them glow brighter than ever they glowed before. For it was the master and not the man who sent the draught through them.

He bade the men good-night and wished them a Merry Christmas, closed the doors, locked them tight, and looked his property over. It was worth being proud of, make no mistake. It was all any man need wish for. It was well stocked and in prime condition. The house, in the cellar of which his smithy stood, was mainly let in lodgings. On the first floor, raised just far enough above the street to give his customers a fair passage out, there was a saloon and eating-room. Back of these were Billy's own rooms, two nice big rooms where his mother took care of him and cooked his meals and washed his clothes and aired his bed as only good old mothers can. Over this floor were two others, let, as I have said, in lodgings—to whom, who knows? Who ever knows to whom lodgings are let in this big, crowded city?

Billy finished his dinner and drew up his chair and one for his mother by the stove, and filled his huge mug with beer, and his huge pipe with tobacco, and talked it all over with his mother. She was a fine woman, was Billy's mother, and she drew a straight, steady rein over her big, burly, good-natured boy. She was Billy's best friend, and he knew it, and when she told him she would stand by and help him, and save for him and look out after him, Billy reached forth his brawny arm, and drew her over on his knee and danced her up and down, smoothing back her gray hair and kissing her old cheeks as if she were a baby.

Then, when the clock struck nine, she got up to wash the dishes, and Billy took his lantern to go down among his forges again. Not that he had anything particular to do, though there never was a time when Billy couldn't find something, but the novelty of owning a business was strong with him, and he wanted to hammer just for the fun of hammering. He descended into the cellar through a side-door which opened from the back hall upon a short ladder. The street doors were barred and bolted. He set his lantern on the ladder steps and lit an oil lamp that hung over his anvil, picked up his iron and his hammer, thrust the one into the coals and laid the other on his anvil, and blew away. Oh, what an arm that was of Billy's! How it made the bellows bulge and the wind roar up the great chimney! How the black coals reddened and flamed and blazed! How the iron glowed and whitened with the heat, and when Billy drew his great hammer down upon it with a hoarse grunt accompanying each blow as if to give it effectiveness, how the sparks scampered about in a furious effort to escape!

OH, WHAT AN ARM WAS THAT OF BILLY'S!

Billy was hammering and grunting at a great rate, and the forge fire was throwing upon the ceiling fantastic illuminations and causing a thousand still more fantastic shadows, when, wholly without preliminary warning or greeting, Billy felt a slight touch on his arm. It was a slight touch, as I said, but a cold one, a very cold one indeed. Billy turned swiftly around with his hammer in one hand and his red-hot iron in the other. Standing almost beside him, with the glare of the fire working a curiously weird effect upon one-half of him, while the other half was almost hidden in the dense shadow beyond, was a tall, spare, angular man with queer little snappy eyes that flashed like diamonds in the light of the forge. His hand was stretched out in a friendly way, and a bland smile stretched across his face, following the lines of his wide, extended lips.

"Aha!" he said cheerily, "how d'ye do? But I forgot! You don't know me and I don't know you. Awkward, eh? But soon fixed, soon fixed. My name's Wrangler, and yours is—er—what by the way, is yours?"

"Warlock," said Billy, laying down his iron and his hammer, and gazing amiably at the stranger—"Billy Warlock."

"Warlock," Mr. Wrangler repeated. "Exactly. Well, then, Warlock, Wrangler. Wrangler, Warlock. And now the formalities have been observed. I don't know how it is with you, Warlock, but I'm a great stickler for the formalities. 'Pon my life, I consider them the web upon which the social fabric hangs together. They're not to be dispensed with upon any account whatever. While I was abroad recently, the American Minister and I were walking along the Mall together. 'Ah,' he suddenly said, 'My dear Wrangler, here comes the Prince. Of course you know him.' Now, it so happened that H. R. H. and I had never met. I didn't have time to reply, for just as I was about to speak the Prince stopped us, and, after greeting the Minister, utterly regardless of the formalities, he told me that he hoped he saw me well. I gave him a look, Warlock, my boy, that he will never forget, and coldly replying, 'Sir, I have not the pleasure of your acquaintance,' I walked on. That afternoon the Minister sent me an apology, but for which damme if I'd ever have spoken to him again."

"AHA!" HE SAID CHEERILY, "HOW D'YE DO?"

During this speech, to which Billy listened with great attention and some little awe, he examined Mr. Wrangler carefully. Mr. Wrangler's clothes were harmoniously seedy. In the degree of their wornness his hat was a match for his coat, and his coat a match for his trowsers, and his trowsers a match for his boots. Although the weather was desperately cold, and a heavy Christmas snow had fallen, he had on neither overcoat nor overshoes. He did not appear to notice Billy's inspecting glances, but having caught his breath, he went cheerily on.

"I am glad and proud to know you, Warlock, old fellow, and I want you to be glad and proud to know me. And you shall be; you shall be; 'gad you sha'n't be able to help it. And you'll find as you know me better that while you won't know any great good of me, you won't know any great harm."

Billy contemplated Mr. Wrangler for a few moments more, and then amiably replied: "Well, that's all right. What more could a man ask?"

"Precisely so," answered Mr. Wrangler, dusting off the anvil and sitting down upon it. "That, I take it, is quite enough. I have not broken in upon your privacy, Warlock, old fellow, without serious occasion. In fact, I'm troubled—sorely troubled."

"I'm sorry for that," said Billy.

"Of course you are, dear boy, and well you may be. The trouble I'm in is a sad one—sad and novel. Not that trouble in itself is a strange experience to me, for I've had my ups and downs. My life hasn't been one of unmixed gayety, I assure you, not by a long shot. But, you see, I have a habit of bowing to the inscrutable will of Providence. Some people experience a great deal of difficulty finding out what the inscrutable will of Providence is. That doesn't bother me in the least. Having ascertained what my own will is, I know the chances are ten to one that the Providential will is exactly the reverse. That is simple and direct enough, isn't it?"

Billy was very much interested in this glib but melancholy stranger, and he resolved, if it came in his way, that he would do the man a favor. So he turned his hammer with the handle to the ground, sat himself upon the head of it, and remarked: "It's right enough, Mr. Wrangler, to make the Lord's will yours. I try to do my best in that line too. But still, there is a point, you know, where it comes hard."

"True, dear boy, very true; and how much harder it is to find yourself in a situation which you did nothing to bring about, for which you are in no sense responsible, which is wholly in conflict with your own will, and to the best of your belief with the will of Providence also! This is my unparalleled situation at this particular moment, and it all comes of being the uncle of a little girl baby."

"No?" said Billy inquiringly, "you don't mean it?"

"I knew you'd be surprised," said Mr. Wrangler, edging up to the forge, which Billy had kept going at a gentle heat to warm their hands now and then. "It ought to be an occasion of unalloyed happiness to be the uncle of a little girl baby. But I was not intended for such a position. It was clearly a mistake to thrust me into it."

"I don't scarcely see how you could help it," said Billy.

"No, I couldn't, could I? It came upon me suddenly and without my knowing it. I had no time for preparation. My brother, who was one of the evils to which, under the will of Providence, I have bowed, called me to him recently, and without so much as a drop of brandy to break the force of the blow, he said: 'Cephas,' said he, 'you are the uncle of a little girl baby!'

"Pale and for a moment speechless, I leaned against the wall and shook with emotion. 'Courage, old man!' said he, 'bear up! bear up!' At first I refused to believe him. 'It is false, Orlando,' I said, 'it can't be so.' But he shook his head sadly. 'It is true, Cephas,' he replied, 'and I guess I ought to know.' That argument was of course conclusive. It admitted of no reply. I only asked him how could he so have wronged me. He said nothing in defense of himself. He could say nothing. He simply bent his head and cried for pardon."

"Well, well," said Billy, "this is queer. It seems to me like a big to-do over a very little matter."

Mr. Wrangler looked up with an expression of dismay. "Little!" he cried. "Little! May I ask, Mr. Warlock, if you have ever been the uncle of a little girl baby?"

"No," said Billy, "I never was."

"Ah, well, that explains it. Then you can't know the bitterness of that hour. You can't put yourself in my place. I forgave him. I told him with a sob that it was all right. Then, in the name of our mother, he implored me to do him a favor. The infant was in California. He had left it there to—er—learn the language, I reckon. He bade me go and fetch it. At first I hesitated—all but refused. But who can withstand an appeal made in the name of his mother? I pressed his hand in silent acquiescence and took the next train West. I found the child and folded it to my heart. I bought it a milk bottle with a fancy nozzle, a bull's eye, and a rattle. It wept, and I dried its tears. Then I brought it back with me. Fancy my feelings, Warlock; picture to yourself my lacerated, bleeding heart, when upon reaching town this afternoon I learned that my brother was dead! Yes, Warlock, old man, dead and buried and cold in his grave, and another party living in his flat. It was all in vain that the tears streamed from my eyes—all in vain that I begged him at least to take the child. I called him brother, kinsman, royal Wrangler, and bade him remember that this was a matter of honor between him and me. I begged him to think of the situation he had placed me in, for I feared the laugh of callous cynics as much as the cry of the innocent child, but the ungrateful dead answered not."

Mr. Wrangler paused and touched his handkerchief to his eyes, while Billy gazed at him in amazement, uncertain to what category of disease his case should be assigned. "I don't know as I ever heard a queerer tale than this," he said at length. "What did you do about it?"

"I'm doing now," answered Mr. Wrangler. "It is on a special mission that I'm seeking you. Warlock, dear boy, you don't happen to have a bottle of paregoric with you, do you, now?"

"Paregoric!" exclaimed Billy. "Why, is the child sick?"

"Hanged if I know!" Mr. Wrangler replied, with evident sincerity. "I'm not what you'd call a connoisseur in infantile disorders, but I guess she's sick. Anyhow, something's the matter. It may be malaria, or chills, or measles, or whooping-cough, or Bright's disease. But whatever it is, it keeps her very wakeful at night. It disturbs her rest sadly. That might, perhaps, be overlooked; but as an intimate consequence it also disturbs mine. At first I supposed it was because she did not get enough nourishment, so, as she wouldn't drink any more milk from her bottle, I bought a syringe, and filling it with milk, I played it down the little darling's throat."

"Great Scott!" cried Billy, "it's a wonder she didn't choke to death!"

"Is it?" asked Mr. Wrangler innocently. "Well, to tell the truth, she did come dev'lish near it, and so I inferred that I hadn't correctly diagnosed the case. After she had got done coughing her spirits seemed more than ever depressed. I went to bed in the vain hope that her supply of tears would in time become exhausted. As the hours drew along and that hope died away, I concluded she must have headache. I had one, and I thought it only natural that she should, too. The question was, what remedy should I apply? In a happy moment paregoric occurred to me. I seemed indistinctly to remember that when I was a child paregoric did the business. How fortunate one is, dear boy, in such moments as that to have the memories of his boyhood to fall back on. I got up, dressed, and went out to hunt a drug-store. Unfortunately, the only two I came across were closed. I returned disconsolate, but as I entered I heard the sound of your hammer and saw the glimmer of the lantern on your ladder. I descended hither. I looked upon you and said: 'Here is a friend.' Warlock, old fellow, find me some paregoric!"

"I don't know much about babies, Mr. Wrangler," said Billy, slowly and rather sternly, "for I never had one, and I never was throwed with 'em. But I think the chances is that you'll kill your'n before morning."

Mr. Wrangler was standing in the shadows where Billy couldn't see him very well, but his snappy little eyes were shining in a way that Billy didn't like.

"How old is the baby?" asked Billy.

"I haven't an idea—not one," answered Mr. Wrangler, laughing merrily, as if his not knowing were a monstrous joke. "But she can walk and talk."

"And you trying to feed her on milk in a bottle?" exclaimed Billy. "How'd you like to be fed on iron filings? I rather think they'd make a good diet for you!" Billy was indignant, and he fetched his hammer down on a log that lay near with a blow that split it through and through. Mr. Wrangler stepped back into the shadows still further, and his little eyes glowed in the darkness like a cat's.

"Ha! ha!" he laughed; "good, very good. But you mustn't make fun of me, old fellow. It isn't fair, now, really."

"Where is the child, anyhow?"

"Upstairs."

"Here, in this house?"

"Precisely."

"Come on, then; take me to her, and let's see what the matter is."

"That's a good fellow!" cried Mr. Wrangler. "As soon as I saw you I knew you would prove to be my deliverer. Come."

The forge fire had now gone out, and directing Mr. Wrangler to stand on top of the ladder, Billy took the lantern, blew out the hanging lamp, and both ascended from the smithy into the hall of the house. Billy locked the door behind him and followed Mr. Wrangler upstairs into the third story. They paused before the hall bedroom and bent forward to listen. Not a sound broke the night's stillness, and softly Mr. Wrangler turned the key and opened the door. Billy moved noiselessly ahead and lit the dull gas.

Upon the bed, with one hand under her cheek and the other one, small and dotted with dimples, resting lightly on her plump neck, lay as pretty a child as he had ever seen. Her eyes were closed, for she was sleeping heavily, as if repose had come to her only when her little frame was utterly worn out. A great mass of thick, tangled curls clustered on the pillow about her head. A dark line down her flushed cheek marked the course of the tears she had been shedding, and the pillow that supported her was still wet with them.

Billy stooped down and kissed her parted lips and her white forehead, while Mr. Wrangler, leaning jauntily against the door, hummed in low strains a melodious lullaby.

"Nothing ails this child," said Billy, when the sound of Mr. Wrangler's voice had died away. "Nothing at all."

UPON THE BED LAY AS PRETTY A CHILD AS HE HAD EVER SEEN.

"Warlock, dear boy," replied Wrangler, "I think you told me you had never been an uncle. The man who has not drank the bitter waters of an uncle's experience for himself is--pardon me, but I must say it—wholly incompetent to speak as to the woes of childhood. How often have you wooed sleep amid the wailings of an infant voice? I'm disappointed in you, Warlock!"

"Don't talk so loud, you'll waken her."

"Spare us that. Let me have my hat and stick. I'll get that paregoric if I have to commit burglary!" and Mr. Wrangler started back as if fully prepared to carry out his threat.

"Be quiet," said Billy, "and look here. My rooms are downstairs where I live with my mother. It's too cold in here for the child. That's one thing that ails her. I'll take her down with me, and when she's had her breakfast in the morning, you can come for her."

Mr. Wrangler seized Billy's hand and shook it fervently. "Dear boy," he said, "you're the kind of a friend to have. Take her and give her a good night's rest."

Billy leaned over the bed, lifted the soundly sleeping child tenderly in his big arms and, followed by Mr. Wrangler, he carried her down to his own room and deposited her upon the bed. Then he turned to Wrangler.

"You'll come for her in the morning, you know?" he said.

HE CARRIED HER DOWN TO HIS OWN ROOM.

"Certainly, old fellow. Good-night, I must get some sleep."

"Good-night," said Billy, "and a Merry Christmas to you."

Mr. Wrangler waved his hand with a grand farewell flourish, blew a kiss toward the little form upon the bed, and passed out into the hall. He waited there an instant, as if undecided what course to pursue. Then he ran upstairs to the hall room, hurriedly crowded his personal effects that lay scattered around the room into his valise, and ran down again into the street. The front door closed with a sharp bang behind him, and he quickly disappeared in the snowy night.

Billy could not help confessing to a sense of relief when his curious new acquaintance left him. Not that he felt any definite fear of Mr. Wrangler. The human being had yet to be born of whom Billy Warlock was afraid. But there was a something about Mr. Wrangler that he didn't fancy. "It's them eyes," said Billy "and he don't make no noise when he walks." His own bed being occupied by the child, he piled a lot of blankets on the floor, stretched himself upon them, and was soon asleep.

The Christmas sun was peeping obliquely into Billy's room and making, with the aid of his shaving-glass, all sorts of fantastic colors on the wall, when a slight tug at the blankets which covered him moved him to start, turn over, open his eyes, stare blankly before him, shut them, open them again, rub them desperately, and finally gaze with awakened consciousness up at the object which had disturbed his slumbers. She was leaning half over the bed, her little fat arms, shoulders, and throat all bare, her bright, tangled hair knotted in bewildering confusion all about her head, and her big blue eyes looking down upon him with a curious interest. How long she had been awake he could only conjecture, but evidently her patience had at last been exhausted, and she had set about premeditatedly to arouse him. Billy was charmed by the little-picture above him, and smiled a cheery greeting. She smiled too, right merrily, and said, "What's your name?"

"Billy," said he. "What's yours?"

The smile straightway faded from her face like the color from a withered blossom, and she glanced hurriedly and anxiously around the room.

"Where's the black man!" she whispered.

"The black man!" cried Billy. "What black man, my dear?"

"Don't you know him? He's had me ever so long."

Billy was puzzled. "A black man had you?" he repeated. "Why you don't mean your uncle, do you?"

"Yes," she said, "that's him, and he says if I don't call him 'uncle' he'll cut off my big toe!"

Billy Warlock jumped upon his feet like a shot. "The devil he did!" he cried. "I'll punch his head for that!"

"And his knife has got six cutters in it!"

"I guess he was only funning," said Billy. "He didn't mean it."

"That's what he said," she insisted.

"Yes, my dear, but he didn't mean it. He was joking."

"That's what he said!" Her accent was very positive, and she added as if conning it over, "His knife had six cutters."

Billy felt himself somewhat at a loss to deal with this well-formed impression, so he contented himself with the remark, "But you haven't told me what your name is yet?"

She rose upon her knees in the bed and leaned over toward him. "My really name is Lotchen."

"Lotchen what?"

"That's all—just Lotchen."

"Where's your mother, Lotchen?"

"I don't know; do you?"

"There's something queer about this business," said Billy to himself. "And if that Wrangler man don't make it plain he'll find hisself in trouble. What is your father's name, Lotchen?" he inquired aloud.

"Who's that?"

"Your father. Haven't you a father?"

"I don't know. The black man says he can turn me into a toothpick if he wants to."

Billy doubled up his fist and looked at it grimly.

"Well, he won't want to," he said. "Don't you be afraid. I'll take care of you."

"Oh, will you?"

"For a little while, anyhow."

"How long?"

"Well, till you get your breakfast."

"Where's he gone?"

"Who?"

"The black man."

"He's upstairs in his room. You can go to him after breakfast."

"I don't want to go. I'm afraid of his knife. I sit and hold on my big toe all day. Have you got a knife, too?" She looked at him with an expression he could not understand. Perhaps her natural trust in mankind had been somewhat shaken.

"My knife wont hurt you," he said. Lotchen crawled to the edge of the bed, leaned over and put her two hands on his, and said, "Then let's you and me run away from the black man."

Billy looked much amused. "No," he replied, "we won't do that, Lotchen; but I shouldn't wonder if he was to run away from us. Don't your uncle love you?"

"He loves his nose better," she replied.

"His which?"

"His nose. He's all the time rubbing it up and down."

"But don't he love you, too?"

"No."

"What makes you think that?"

"'Cause I'm afraid of him."

"When did you see him first, Lotchen?"

"Oh, ever so long. He's had me, you know."

"Yes, I know that. What's he been doing with you?"

The expression on her face was so blank that Billy saw, whatever Mr. Wrangler might intend, she knew nothing more than that she was being "had" under circumstances that caused her constant fright. He did not question her further, but went into the kitchen where his mother was getting the griddle hot for the buckwheat cakes and the spider hot for the sausages, and he told her of Wrangler and the child. She went in to see Lotchen, and snuggled the little one up to her close and tight, and told her she should have a merry Christmas and she mustn't be afraid of anybody, for her Billy, that is, Billy's mother's Billy, could whip anybody on earth, she didn't care who he was, and nobody should frighten this dear little soul; and the old lady began now to express her ideas in that strange language which is hidden from the wise and prudent but revealed unto grandmammas and babes. "B'essings!" she said, "b'essings on 'e dear heart an' e' 'ittie body, wiv 'e 'ittie youn' nose, an' 'e ittie b'u' eyes, an' 'e ittie youn' cheeks, an' e' ittie youn' evysing, an' nobody s'all bozzer her at all, not 'e 'east ittie bit, 'tause s'e was a sweet ittie fwing, and Billy, wiz him big fist an' him date big arm, Billy dust take 'e b'ack mans an' all 'e uzzer mans wot bozzer zis ittie soul an' 'e frow 'em yite in 'e Norf Yiver, yite in, not carin' 'tall bout 'e ice, but dus' frow 'em in an' yet 'em det out e' bes' way zay tan. B'ess ittie heart!"

Then Lotchen smiled and put up her pretty face to be kissed, which she didn't have to do twice before it was kissed by them both, and Billy who hadn't slung hammers all his life for nothing, rolled up his shirt-sleeves and doubled up his fists, and sparred away at the air as if to suggest what would happen to any one who laid as much as his little finger on her.

All through the breakfast Billy kept his eyes on that round, pretty face, and wondered what he should say and do when the "black man" came to get her. He began to grow moody and sullen as the buckwheat cakes disappeared, and when thirty of them had been disposed of Billy felt himself ready to meet Mr. Wrangler. He had some questions he desired to ask Mr. Wrangler, and the oftener he thought them over the more he felt his fingers itch to close themselves around Mr. Wrangler's long and scraggy neck. He waited an hour, two hours, but no Mr. Wrangler came, and at last Billy concluded to mount the stairs and to interview Mr. Wrangler in the hall bedroom.

He told Lotchen to go into his room, where she had spent the night, and on her assuring him that she wasn't afraid, he locked her in and stowed the key away in his pocket. Then he shot upstairs to the hall bedroom. He knocked, but no answer came. He opened the door. The room was empty. The bed was just as he had left it the night before with the impression upon it of the little form he had carried away. It had evidently been without a tenant during the night. All that Christmas Day he waited and watched for Mr. Wrangler, but he waited and watched in vain.

Two days afterward an express wagon drew up before the smithy, and a box was delivered to Billy marked with his name. It contained a liberal supply of child's clothing, which Lotchen recognized as hers. Little by little Billy and his mother drew from her fragments of her history. She remembered a big house by the water, and a little bed of lilies-of-the-valley under a couple of pear-trees. She remembered a colored man named Pete, but there was no response in her memory to the words "father" and "mother," and the only woman who appeared to be impressed on her mind was one who called her "Lassie" and gave her horrid stuff from a bottle in a wooden spoon.

Days and weeks and years went on, and Billy Warlock's purse grew plumper and his heart grew lighter with each of them. His smithy in the cellar grew in dimensions and gradually he absorbed the little old house over it. The saloon disappeared, and the room it had occupied became a parlor for Lotchen. The lodgers went out one by one until the whole house was Billy's dwelling.

One day when she was nearly fourteen years old, Billy received a letter that worried him a good deal. It was dated at the Newcastle Jail in Delaware. It read:

MY DEAR WARLOCK:

It seems to be definitely settled about my being an error of judgment. You can see by the enclosed newspaper clipping that I ought not to have been involved in the scheme of the creation. You needn't mention it to anybody else. I forget what name you knew me by, but I think it was

The newspaper clipping contained these words:

Nothing, therefore, remains for the Court but to pronounce the sentence which a jury, almost wholly of your own selection, has adjudged your fitting doom. The crime you have committed is the most dreadful known to the law. For it there is but one penalty, the requisition of your life in forfeit for the one you have taken. The sentence of the Court is that you be conducted hence to the prison from which you came, and that you be confined there until Friday, the 18th day of March, following, and that you then, between the hours of 7 and 11 in the morning, be hanged by the neck until you are dead, and may God have mercy on you!

This is all that Billy Warlock knows or cares to know of the circumstances under which Lotchen became his child. He never made the slightest effort to discover more. It didn't interest him, and he didn't wish it to interest her. She was his child, and that was enough—at least, it was enough for several years. The precise moment at which it ceased to be enough is not fixed in Billy's mind, but last Christmas, when Lotchen found a gold watch in her stocking, and when she came and put her arms around his neck and kissed him, which she hadn't done very often of late, and when she whispered that she wished she had something to give him, Billy turned his eyes to the floor and stuck his big fists in his trowsers pockets, and did a power of thinking. He knew then, if he had not fully known it before, that for her to be his child was not enough. So he said very solemnly, "Are you sure you mean that, Lotchen? Now, don't answer without you know, for you might have something you wouldn't want to give me, and if I was to ask for it and you was to look hesitatin', I—well I don't know what I should do."

"I don't have to think, Billy," Lotchen answered promptly, "for I've been thinking a great deal and wondering whether you—"

She stopped there short, and her face—her pretty face, her dear, round, dimpled face, her truthful, honest, womanly face—got very red, and she jumped up and ran out of the room.

After that last Christmas, Billy and Lotchen talked and walked with each other on a different footing from that on which their intercourse had previously been conducted. He said nothing to her, nor she to him, that referred to their interrupted conversation until October came, and then one day he said: "Lotchen, is my Christmas gift ready?" and he held out his hand to her—both hands—and smiled.

"Yes, Billy," she answered.

And on next Tuesday morning, Christmas morning, when the bells are ringing merrily and all the world is glad, Billy Warlock, as I said at the very beginning of my story, dressed in his big frock coat and the whitest of snowy neckties, will—but you know the rest, so what's the use of my telling it?

MR. CINCH.

In the construction of Mr. Cinch nature had been generous, not to say prodigal, of materials, but certainly a wiser discretion might have been exercised in using them. The centre of Mr. Cinch's gravity was much too far above his waist. All the rest of him appeared to have been fitted out at the expense of his legs, which, unable to endure so oppressive a burden, had spread.

To say that the shape of his legs was a source of unhappiness to Mr. Cinch would be a feeble and inadequate expression of his feelings. "Them bow-legs" was a phrase into which he poured a degree of self-contempt altogether pitiful. They were, of course, homely to look at and not in the least serviceable. Unaided by his stout hickory stick, they could not transport Mr. Cinch across the room. But there was no evidence that their shape or size was due on their part to any motive of malice or of indolence, and it seemed quite unreasonable that he should feel toward them so harshly.

His disgust for them did not, indeed, originate with himself. It is entirely probable that he would never have thought of despising them as he did but for Mrs. Cinch. That excellent lady, with all her many virtues, could never forgive those legs. Their degeneration, as she regarded it, had not begun when she married Mr. Cinch. He was then a slight young man and his legs were unexceptionable in size and shape. They had become bowed and insufficient within comparatively recent years, and she had never felt quite able to accept Mr. Cinch's assurances that he was not at fault in the matter.

Let it not be thought that this excellent couple were wanting toward each other in those sweet graces which so beautify the marriage relation. They had lived and loved together nearly a quarter of a century, and had shared in those years their full measure of joys and sorrows. But Mrs. Cinch was not without her humors, and when she was entertaining an acid humor she could not get her husband's unfortunate legs out of her mind.

No matter what may have been the subject that had originally vexed her, it was the invariable experience that those legs became the focus to which her excited wrath was drawn, and then, indeed, it must be owned, she was exceedingly hard to deal with. She would recall in bitter phrases the fact that he had married her with other and honester legs, and she would plainly intimate that in substituting these he had acted in an unfair and unmanly way.

This was naturally distressing to Mr. Cinch. He keenly felt the injustice of the insinuation, but at the same time his mind was filled with a supreme loathing of his legs, and he was only deterred from going to a hospital and from having them straightway taken off by the reflection that an entirely legless husband was not likely to be more satisfactory, upon the whole, than one whose legs were bowed.

It was from a domestic scene such as these sentences have indicated that Mr. Cinch issued one morning recently, and passing out through his hallway into the street as fast as he could wobble, he tumbled into his waiting coupé and hurried down to business. Mr. Cinch was the keeper of a livery-stable, an establishment held in much esteem by the public and the trade, and yielding an abundant revenue. His business was one of the largest of its kind in New York, a fact which, with many others equally important, was set forth in unmistakable phrases upon Mr. Cinch's business cards, copiously illustrated with cuts of prancing horses and handsome vehicles and of the extensive premises in which they were kept.

The appearance of the coupé as it rolled into the stable fetched from the inner office Mr. Cinch's manager, a bald-headed young man, with red eyes and a hopeful soul, who dexterously assisted his employer to alight, and aided him into the main office and into the huge arm-chair, so placed as to command a fair view of the entire establishment. From this arm-chair, Mr. Cinch rarely moved throughout the live-long day.

"Well, Bob," said Mr. Cinch, so soon as he had caught his breath, "how's things going?"

"Fair to middlin', sir, fair to middlin'. The regulars is 'bout the same, but the casuals is light."

"Well, a man can't always have things the way he wants 'em, Bob; ef he could there wouldn't be as much trouble as they is."

"No, sir, that's very true, sir, nor so much fun, neither, come to think of it."

"How do you make that out, Bob?"

"Well, sir, ef everybody could have whatever they wanted, there wouldn't be much excitement going on. They'd get tired o' wanting before long fearful that the time 'ud come when they wouldn't be nothin' to want."

Mr. Cinch was quite impressed with the force of this philosophy. Bob's views on men and things often entertained Mr. Cinch. He had a good deal of respect for Bob. Bob's circumstances had denied him many of those early advantages which are so useful in cultivating the habit of profound thought, and yet, to his greater credit, it must be said that he not infrequently performed a deal of subtle cogitation. In this he pleased Mr. Cinch, who was by no means all a man of beef and brawn. Mr. Cinch had read a considerable quantity of poetry and was a subscriber to a scientific periodical. He had a decided tendency toward occult speculation, and had reached that point in his orthodoxy where he believed there were a good many more things that we don't know than that we do.

He had turned over Bob's remark once or twice in his mind, and was about to say something by way of rejoinder when the office door was opened and a young woman entered, observing that she wished to pay her bill.

She was a tall, well-dressed, stoutly built young woman, with large, strong features, and an abundant supply of blonde hair, partially covered with a sombre brown bonnet. Her eyes were big and blue, and her voice quite pleasant to hear.

"This way, miss," said Bob, from his high stool behind the desk. "What name, please?"

"Frances Emiline Beeks."

"Beeks, miss? Yes, miss. Let's see—BA to BE, Barker, Becker, Beech, Beeks! Frances Emiline Beeks. Eighty-seven dollars and fifty cents, if you please."

"That seems like a good deal of money," observed Miss Beeks.

"Well, now, it is, miss," said Bob. "But you use a kerridge a good deal, miss, mostly every day and sometimes oftener. You've called more this month than ever. Why don't you keep a hoss, miss? That ud be the cheapest."

"It certainly would if my bills are to run up like this. However, I'm too busy now to talk about it. Let me have your pen while I fill out this check. There— is that right?"

"Yes, miss, thank you. I think that sorrel would suit you nicely. He's only—"

"Well, I'll think it over. Good-morning!"

Miss Beeks went out and Mr. Cinch, who had been regarding her over his glasses, inquired, "Who's the young woman, Bob?"

"I don't know, sir, hardly," said Bob, "but I think she's some kind of a doctor."

"She seems to be makin' pretty good bills."

"And they gets better all the time. Whatever she doctors, it's a good business, for she pays her bill the day after she gets it every time."

"What makes you think she doctors?"

"She said so, as near as I could make out. She come in here one day last month—it was when I had that staving big bile on my elbow, you remember?"

"Yes."

"Well, I was settin' here huggin' that bile, and it was just thumpin'. Seemed to me 's if they was a whole bag o' carpet-tacks stuck in that arm. I was so used up I couldn't walk around, and so stuck full of pain I couldn't set still. Well, 's I said, she come in and ordered a coach, and while it was being fetched around she give me a look and she says, 'What's the matter?' I says 'I got a bile.'

"'A what?' says she.

"'A bile,' says I.

"'Oh, no,' says she.

"'Well, if you don't think so,' says I, 'look there,' says I, and I prodooced the bile, which 'peared to me to be pretty good evidence.

"She looked at it and then says, as cool as you please, 'Well, what of it?'

"'A WHAT?' SAYS SHE. 'A BILE?' SAYS I.'"

"'Don't you call that a bile?' says I, 'and if you don't think it hurts you'd better.' You see, bein' nearly crazy with the hurts of it, and her so unconcernin', I thought she was workin' a guy on me. But she says, 'I see what you call a bile, and maybe you think it hurts, but I know it don't. Why, what is it?' says she; 'it's nothing but a little lump of red flesh. It don't hurt.

It can't hurt. How can it? Flesh don't live any more than wood or stone, and if it don't live, how can it feel? It's you that feels and hurts, and you have made yourself believe it's this little lump of red flesh, and you've gone and painted it and greased it and wrapped it up and fooled with it when there's nothing the matter with it, and everything the matter with you.' That's what she said, looking me dead in the eyes."

Mr. Cinch had grown very much interested in Bob's account of this peculiar conversation. As Bob went on he had screwed around in his arm-chair, and had drawn his brow into a reflective knot.

"I don't know as I understand what that means, Bob," he observed, cautiously.

"It took me a good while to get it through me," replied the manager, "but I think I see what she was driving at. She means that a man's body is just like any other matter and don't make feelings, and that's it's his soul that does the feeling, and that when his soul feels bad he says he has a bile or the colic or the rheumatism, and begins to put on plasters and take pills when he ought not to do anything of the kind, but ought to talk to her and get her to cure his soul. That's the way she give it to me, anyhow. She talked here for half an hour. She said that it was silly to set your feelings down to this or that place in your body. She said she could talk to me awhile about the—er, let's see, gravity, no, yes, gravi—oh, I know! about the gravitation of the soul, and my feelings would get good and the bile go down."

"Oh, rats!" remarked Mr. Cinch.

"Well, I don't know, sir," replied Bob, doubtfully. "I don't know but what I think there is something in it?"

"Stuff! Bob, how kin there be? Do you mean that she made out 'at she could cure anything by just talking to you?"

"Not exactly; no sir. Her p'int is that what we call biles or malaria, or—"

"Bow-legs, mebbe," put in Mr. Cinch both jocosely and ruefully.

"Yes, sir, bow-legs."

"What!"

"Bow-legs, too—why not? Just as easy bow-legs as biles."

"Well, go on."

"All such things, she says, is appearances. Our souls being sick, they look through our eyes in a sorter cock-eyed way and see something they call a bile or a pair of bow-legs. The bile and the bow-legs aint really there, you know; we only think so, which is just as bad as if they was there. If we was to go to her and get our souls well, we'd look out of our eyes straight and wouldn't see no bile or bow-legs. Neither would nobody else. This is the best explaining I can do, sir. I understands it pretty well, but I can't talk it. She's a daisy talker, though. She can talk like a dictionary."

"Bob," said Mr. Cinch, solemnly, "do you mean to tell me that this young woman can talk me into believing that I aint got bow-legs?"

Bob hesitated. He looked at Mr. Cinch long and seriously. Mr. Cinch took up his walking-stick and slowly lifted himself upon his feet.

"Look at them legs, Bob. You can shove a prize punkin through 'em without touching. Can this young woman make me believe them legs is straight? If she can, Bob, if she can, she don't need to buy no hoss, nor pay no coach-hire any more."

The responsibility of this awful moment was too much for Bob. "If I was you," he said discreetly, "I'd talk to her about it the next time she comes in."

"LOOK AT THEM LEGS, BOB!"

Mr. Cinch made no reply, but he continued for several minutes to look ruefully down where he believed his legs to be, and then he resumed his chair. Bob returned to his accounts and a heavy tide of business flowed in to engage their attention. Business was always well done in Mr. Cinch's office, and it suffered that morning no more than on any other morning, and yet there was a certain influence in the room which seemed to be affecting both him and Bob. They talked together less than usual and in addressing others were short and sharp. When Bob got off his stool and said he was going to luncheon he broke a silence which might almost be called ominous.

He was not long gone, but upon his return the office was empty. It was so unusual a circumstance for Mr. Cinch to go out that Bob wondered not a little what had happened. His wonderment increased as the afternoon drew along and Mr. Cinch did not return. Nobody could tell where or when he had gone or in what manner his departure had been effected. He had not made use of his coupé or any other vehicle. No scrap of writing could be found that threw the least light upon so startling a proceeding, nor did any one turn up with whom a message had been left.

Evening approached and numerous misgivings entered Bob's mind. He knew that Mr. Cinch's domestic life was not without moments of bitterness, and he was satisfied that one of them had preceded his appearance at the office that morning. The vague suspicions that crept into his head were strengthened when, just before 6 o'clock, a messenger came from Mrs. Cinch loaded with inquiries. Mr. Cinch's life was as regular as the movements of the stars. He had gone home at 4:30 P.M. for twenty years. Bob was really alarmed. He made a careful search throughout the stables. That failing to give him the slightest clew, he went to see Mrs. Cinch.

When he told that excellent woman that her husband had disappeared, she precipitately swooned away. The unhappy incident of the morning was still fresh in her repentant mind, and she could have no doubt that her over-worried lord had sought in the North River the peace of mind she had denied him in his home. Bob could not comfort her. He could only apply a wet towel to her heated temples and beg her to be calm. This he did with praiseworthy diligence during the greater part of the evening, and when he left it was with the understanding that, if the missing man were not seen or heard from by the next morning, he would notify the police and have them send out a general alarm.

This, indeed, had to be done. Mr. Cinch had disappeared. His affairs were all right, his fortune untouched and no motive anywhere apparent why he should have taken so reckless a step. The police could get no trace of him. Fat and bow-legged men were encountered here, there and everywhere, were seized and sharply questioned, but from none of these incidents of the search was the slightest hope extracted. Two days passed, and still another, but the mystery continued to be dark and impenetrable and Mrs. Cinch was wrapped in an envelope of grief.

Bob's story about Miss Beeks and her novel views had profoundly impressed Mr. Cinch, and being so constituted that when he got hold of an idea he had to give himself up to its consideration, Miss Beeks and the possible effect of her conversation upon his legs kept revolving before his eyes all the morning. He was not able to form any very definite idea of what she might be expected to do, but he thought it quite within the possibilities for her to improve the situation. The notion that in ailments of all kinds there was a large element of imagination had occurred to him frequently when listening to Mrs. Cinch's accounts of her numerous physical tribulations, and he was by no means sure that his legs were as bad as they had been represented. He thought it might well be that he had obtained an exaggerated notion of their deformity, and if Miss Beeks merely succeeded in convincing him of that the gain would be something. He picked up the address-book during the morning and ascertained that she lived in a large apartment-house in Broadway, distant from his stables less than a block. While Bob was at luncheon he got upon his feet, went to the door and looked down the street at the big flat. An irresistible desire to go and talk the matter over with Miss Beeks took possession of him, and almost before he knew it he was seated in a little reception-room waiting for the appearance of the remarkable young woman who professed to be able to talk away a boil.

She did not keep him waiting long, and when she held out her hand and wished him "Good-morning," he was quite captivated with her cheery voice and smile.

Mr. Cinch proceeded directly to business. First he took from his pocket-book one of his large and profusely illustrated business cards and delivered it with something of pride by way of introduction. Then he remarked that he had heard of her and of her way of doctoring and he thought he'd just drop around and see what she could do in his case.

"Why, what ails you?" she asked. "You look very comfortable."

"So I be," replied Mr. Cinch, much gratified, "but it's all along of my legs."

"And what of them?"

"Well you see, they're bowed, and—"

"Don't say what I see, Mr. Cinch. We see with our minds and only through our eyes. My mind is healthy, and as I see your legs there's nothing the matter with them."

"You don't say so!"

"To be sure I do. At the same time if you say your legs are bowed, there is, of course, trouble somewhere."

"Of course," assented Mr. Cinch.

"The question is, where? Some people would say, in the legs. They would try to make you believe that your legs, mere combinations of flesh and blood, could go off by themselves and get bowed, or knock-kneed, or long or short, or slim or fat, or gouty, or palsied, or paralyzed, or rheumatic, or shriveled or anything else just as they wanted to and all of their own option, as though they were a living soul with a living will and not simply so many square inches of inanimate matter. Now, Mr. Cinch, that's all nonsense. Don't you believe a word of it!"

"OUR BODIES ARE BUT GHOSTS," SAID THE SCIENTIST.

"Well, now," replied the old man slowly, "I never thought of it that-away. It don't seem as if they could go and get bowed all of themselves. But," and he looked down toward them dubiously, "they do 'pear to be bowed, now, don't they?"

"Maybe they do. We'll come to that presently. But first let me prove that, if they are bowed, they didn't do it. Suppose you were to have them cut off at your hips, would they go on and bow more?"

"Why, no."

"Of course not," said the Scientist, triumphantly. "That shows they didn't bow themselves. Then who did bow them? I'll tell you. You have done it, Mr. Cinch, you, yourself."

"Mebbe I did, mebbe I did. I won't deny it. But this I will say—that I didn't go for to do it."

"Perhaps not. But, consciously or unconsciously, your mind became—well, for want of a better word, sick. In that sick condition it began to look around for a place in your body to reflect its trouble upon. It chose your legs, and straightway your eyes, prompted by your diseased mind, began to tell you that your legs were bowed."

"Well, really!" cried Mr. Cinch, "how very plain you make it."

"It's plain enough to such as will see. Matter, Mr. Cinch, does not act. Matter has no will. It doesn't feel, or get tired, or wear out or do any of the things attributed to it by thoughtless people. Matter is inanimate and takes form only as the mind, the soul, the Vital Force, wills that it shall. It responds to the soul. Therefore, if your legs are bowed, your mind is at fault."

"What a very uncomfortable thing your mind must be!" said Mr. Cinch. "It's 'most as well not to have none!"

"Better," exclaimed the Scientist, earnestly, "if it is to be out of harmony with the Mind Universal. And now we come to the real point. The thing to cure is the thing that is sick. The bowness of your legs is the reflection of your bowed mind. Straighten your mind and your legs will be as straight as your walking-stick. Shut your eyes, Mr. Cinch, and think only of what I say. Nothing is real except the ideal. The corporeal realm of created being corresponds precisely to the condition of the ideal. Do you see the point?"

"Sorter," replied Mr. Cinch, feebly, "but I b'lieve I could see it better if I was to open my eyes."

"No, no, no!" cried the Scientist. "It is highly necessary to keep them shut and turned inwards."

"I don't b'lieve I can come that, mum," Mr. Cinch rejoined, apologetically. "My eyes is getting a bit old."

"Sink them far into your soul! Look there to find your bad and ugly ideals! Give me your hand, Mr. Cinch. Thus, with our hands clasped, will our spiritual understandings commune. Together we will pursue our investigations into the recesses of your ethereal nature, and with the clean new broom of inspired reason, will we sweep away the dusty cobwebs of bad ideals!"

Mr. Cinch heaved a huge sigh! But he shut his eyes vigorously, and received into his big hard fist the Scientist's little white one, and murmured, "All right, mum; whip up lively."

"Our bodies are but ghosts," said the Scientist, "combinations of symbols. The combinations change as the soul that they symbolize changes. I look at your body and it tells me of your soul. I see a soul full of doubt and darkness, and the doubt and darkness are symbolized in the curved and ugly form of your legs. Brush away the doubt! Dispel the darkness! Aspire toward the Life of the Spirit, and as your aspirations are tenacious they will draw your legs into the shape which, like the spirit it typifies, will be all beauty. Does your soul respond, Mr. Cinch?"

"Well, mum, I dunno. I'm trying hard, but—"

"Ah, there is unbelief there. I see it—a black mountain-cloud of unbelief. Faith, Mr. Cinch, is the ethical law of gravitation. You already feel its influence. It draws you to the Spiritual Center of Essence. Your soul still walks in the shadow, but toward the light. You are being drawn away from the doubt. Don't you feel yourself being drawn, Mr. Cinch?"

"I b'lieve I do, mum; I really b'lieve I do. That left leg give a kinder twitch just as you spoke."

"Of course it did! Of course it did! You are in the sea of Infinite Thought, floating, floating like a chip on the water. The evil ways of falsehood, doubt and unbelief are trying to beat you away from the Current of Truth,—but no! it shall not be! I will stand by to fight them back, and to urge on those other waves that will bear you into the current. One is approaching now— the Wave of Harmony. It touches you gently, lifts you on its crystal bosom, and, ere it leaves to do the same duty to another floating chip, it moves you many paces nearer to the current. And now, as you rest, another comes. Lo, it is intercepted by the discordant ripples of suspicion, and a struggle ensues! But, look! Oh, prythee look! From the white caps of conflict the wave, larger, purer than ever, emerges, and comes on apace. It is the Wave of Joy! It moves quickly! It takes you upon its sparkling crest! Whence the diamond lights of happiness flash! Merrily flash! It heaves you swiftly on! On! On! Ah! Yes! Nearer! Nearer still! One more impulse and you are there! It lifts its glittering form again! And NOW!—Oh, Mr. Cinch! you are in the Current! the CURRENT! Do you not feel its swift influence? The Current of Truth! Brightly, joyously, swiftly does this Spiritual Gulf Stream bear you toward the Great Central Calm! Ah!—ah!"

The Scientist was evidently in a great state of excitement. Her voice had risen to a keen soprano key, and her eyes sparkled wildly. When she had finally succeeded in getting Mr. Cinch into the Current, she fell back in her chair, quite exhausted.

Neither spoke for several minutes, and then Miss Beeks finally said: "Open your eyes, Mr. Cinch!" The old man looked at her with evident curiosity. "You talk beautiful," he said, earnestly, "and I really think I feel better!"

"IT WAS A GOOD DEAL, MR. GROANER."

"Don't say 'feel,' Mr. Cinch. Cultivate thought and not sensation. I know you are better and that means, of course, that the supposititious curvature of your limbs, never real, is less apparent. You must put yourself under my treatment from this moment. The advantage gained already must not be lost. You must not go home, or to business, or out of this room until your mind is thoroughly healed. You must not get out of the Current until you are safely in the Calm Centre."

It was the fourth day after her husband's strange disappearance, and Mrs. Cinch was seated in the back parlor of her desolate house, receiving spiritual consolation from an elderly clerical gentleman. "Oh, sir," she was saying, "he was such a good man, so gentle and easy to get along with. He had no harsh words, no matter how much he had to bear. And I'm fearful it was a good deal, Mr. Groaner, I'm fearful it was a good deal."

Mr. Groaner sighed with much feeling, and said she must not repine, adding in a comforting way that the world was full of sorrow.

"Yes," said Mrs. Cinch, as though greatly consoled by that fact, "I know it. We all have our burdens and I s'pose we need 'em."

"Indeed we do, Sister Cinch," Mr. Groaner replied, "but for our burdens we should grow vain and worldly."

This disastrous result being in Mrs. Cinch's case rendered less menacing through the supposed death of her partner, the good man proceeded to show her the necessity of "bearing up," and of counting all things good, and of drawing from these mournful visitations the valuable lesson that earthly affections are empty and void. Much had been accomplished toward reconciling her to the unhappy situation when a familiar click was heard in the front door latch.

Mrs. Cinch started.

The click was repeated and then the door was flung open, and a heavy footfall sounded in the hallway.

"William!" cried Mrs. Cinch. "It's William, Brother Groaner! Help me up! Help me to run and meet him! William, my dear, good, sweet, bow-legged old William! O, Brother Groaner, I shall go crazy with happiness! Hear his old feet, stuck on them dear bow-legs of his, making a sound that I'd know 'mong ten thousand! Come along, Brother Groaner, come long."

They got into the hall with as much speed as possible, and there, coming toward them was Mr. Cinch, his round face lighted with a peaceful smile. He paused, and there was something in his manner and attitude that caused them to pause as well. He brought his pudgy feet closely together and straightened his figure to its loftiest possibility, as if to call attention to its perfect beauty.

"Maria, my dear," he said, in deep, low tones, "I float in the Calm Centre of Infinite Truth."

A look of profound alarm came upon Mrs. Cinch's face, and she glanced at the Rev. Mr. Groaner. He shook his head sadly.

Mr. Cinch observed the dubious looks and he hastened to dispel them.

"I am in harmony with the Universal Mind," he said. "Look at them legs!"

They looked. "Yes, William," answered Mrs. Cinch, profoundly disturbed, "I see them legs, and dear, sweet, precious old legs they are, William, and if I ever said they wasn't, I told a story and goodness knows I've suffered enough for it in the last three days and nights. I love them cunning old legs, William, better'n all the rest of you put together, and I don't care where you're floating nor what you're in harmony with, I only just know you're back again with the same beautiful, chubby, round old legs you took away, and I'm downright crying happy, and the rounder they gets the more I'll love them!"

And, unable longer to restrain herself, the good old lady rushed upon him and hugged him black and blue.

Mr. Cinch may still be floating in the Calm Centre of Infinite Truth, or he may not. He may still be in harmony with the Universal Mind or he may not. He hasn't mentioned lately. But this is sure truth—that wherever he floats, Mrs. Cinch is floating with him, and whatever else he may be in harmony with he is certainly in harmony with her. He wobbles and toddles up and down just as he used to do, but never a word does he hear to the prejudice of his legs. And whether they be as crooked as a ram's horn or as straight as a rifle-barrel, he can't see them and she won't—so what's the odds, anyhow?

XIII.

GRANDMOTHER CRUNCHER.

Tony Scollop's great point was enterprise. When he looked at anything it was always with the query running through his mind, how can this be turned to account? The beauty of utility was the beauty which Tony's eyes detected and which his heart valued.

There may be a want of true and pure sentiment in this way of considering the world and its contents, but Tony's lot had been cast in a sphere where necessity encroaches upon sentiment. Bread was dear and babies cheap in the tenement where Tony was born, and his character was greatly affected by this circumstance.

And yet Tony was not unmindful of the fact that sentiment is a powerful stimulant. As such, he prized it. His acute perception disclosed to him that people would pay freely to have their sentiments fed, and Tony was willing to do almost anything not specifically mentioned in the Criminal Code, for pay. It had been early impressed upon his mind that the profitable sentiments of a great proportion of mankind were reached through their curiosity. This lesson was first enforced upon Tony by a Monkey.

The monkey was a particularly clever knave. He was in the retinue consisting, besides himself, of a woman, two babies, a hand-organ and a tin-cup, appertaining to a dusky Neapolitan who infested the tenement district in which Tony's boyhood was spent. That monkey had on several occasions seduced a penny from Tony's unwilling hand. Thereby he had earned Tony's respect and had caused Tony's reflections to dwell upon him. That monkey had a large place in the circumstances which led Tony to go into the dime-museum business.

As a dime-museum manager, to which exalted station Tony finally arose and in which he was now engaged, he was a remarkable success. He seemed to have found just the field for his talents. They led him into a great variety of speculations, but from one and all he emerged plethoric with dimes. His museum had grown until it now occupied the three floors of one of the largest buildings in the Bowery.

It was in the very height of his great career, when his enterprise was most conspicuous, his curiosities most numerous, his patronage most extensive, and his self-appreciation most complete and complacent, that he was called upon to face a singular emergency.

A gentleman in Hoboken had boiled his mother-in-law. It is of no moment now why he had boiled his mother-in-law, though at the time the consideration of this question had filled columns upon columns of the daily newspapers. There had been a controversy between the gentleman and his mother-in-law, prolonged and distracting, and the long and short of a very painful conjunction of circumstances is that the gentleman had felt himself reduced to the necessity of doing something serious to his mother-in-law, and, thus moved, he had boiled her. It would have been wiser, doubtless, had he taken some other course, though that is a matter of judgment into which I refrain from going. The only fact needful to be mentioned here is that the event had taken up a vast amount of space in the papers, which had printed large maps of the room wherein the boiling had occurred, together with striking pictures of the gentleman, the mother-in-law, the kettle in which the boiling had been done, the cat which usually slept in the kettle, and other important accessories of the event.

Among these was the gentleman's grand-mother, a venerable lady living in Wisconsin, who, upon being informed that her grandson was in jail for boiling his mother-in-law, had come on to Hoboken to comfort him. She was met at the depot by a considerable company of reporters, and by Mr. Tony Scollop, who, with an enterprise all his own, provided a coach for her, went with her to the jail, remained during the sad interview that took place with her unhappy grandson, and gave her a gorgeous bouquet with which to assuage her grief. He took her to a hotel, and did not leave her until she had signed a ten weeks' contract to appear in his dime museum. These, with many other facts illustrative of Tony's generosity and gentle sympathy, appeared in many of the newspapers the next day.

Whatever may have been their general effect, there were bosoms in which they produced disagreeable sensations, and among these was the bosom of Billy O'Fake, the Wild Man from Borneo. Indeed Mr. O'Fake was positively angry when he saw that Grandmother Cruncher was to be exhibited from the same platform with himself. He stuck his pipe in his mouth, his hat on his head, and his feet on the footboard of his bed, and said emphatically that he be domned if he'd shtand the loikes av this gran'mother business any more at all. It had gone the laste bit too fur, an', bedad, he'd lay the hull matter before the Brotherhood and Sisterhood of Animated Frakes that blissid marnin'!

The more Mr. O'Fake thought it over the more outraged his feelings became. At last, unable longer to contain himself, he strode from his room, descended into the Bowery, passed into East Broadway, and clambered aloft to the fifth story of a rickety flat. There he knocked loudly at a door and responded in something of violent haste to the invitation to enter.

Seated in one corner of the room, over a small, red-hot stove, was a queer-looking little man. There was a tin plate on the stove from which the odor of melting cheese arose, and mingling with the odor of burning tobacco, contributed from the little man's pipe, burdened the atmosphere with dense and by no means delightful fumes. The little man had a fork in one hand and a mug of beer in the other and he was snatching the cheese from the plate, shoving it into his mouth and washing it down with the beer at a rate and with a disregard of heat and cold that were wonderful to observe.

"SIT, IS IT? WHERE?" SAID BILLY.

He was anything but a pretty little man. His head was big and his body small and his legs very short and very thick. He sat upon a keg, the top of which he quite amply covered, but his feet came scarcely half-way to the floor. His gray eyes twinkled from holes sunk far into his head, and twinkled so brightly that you had to look at them, but so sharply that you wouldn't if you could have helped it. He peeked quickly at Mr. O'Fake, and cried in a shrill voice:

"Hi! hi! Billy! Come in an' sit down!"

"Sit, is it? Where?" said Billy.

"Vhere?" repeated the queer little man. "If I vos to tell you vhere, Billy, your hingenuity vouldn't be drored out. Von o' the uses of hexperience, Billy, is to dror hout the hingenuity. You're lookin' summat doleful, Billy. Cheer hup, me boy, cheer hup! I'd like to inwite you to this 'ere feast, but there's honly von 'elp o' cheese left, an' honly von svaller of beer. But pull hout yer pipe an'—vot's on yer mind, Billy?"

Mr. O'Fake was standing with his back against the door, his arms folded, his hat on the side of his head, and an ominous expression on his face.

"Have ye seen the marnin' papers, Runty?" he inquired.

"Papers, Billy, papers? Vot do I vant wid the papers. No, Billy, I shuns 'em. No man can be a 'abitchual reader huv the papers, Billy, vidout comin' to a bad hend."

Mr. O'Fake drew from his pocket a copy of "The Daily Bazoo," and pointing at a certain paragraph, said: "Rade thot, Runty!"

The queer little man stuck his fork under the tin plate and flipped it off the stove upon the floor, heedless of Mr. O'Fake's wishes. "Hexcuse me, Billy," he said, "I never wiolate my princerples. I 'ave no use for papers an' I never reads 'em. Wot's it say?"

"Bedad, I'll tell ye pwhat it says. It says outrage. It says another wan o' thim ould women has come bechune me an' me daily bread. It says that Tony Scollop's been and hired some ould hag av a gran'mother to shtep in an' discredit the perfession. I was a lad av tin years, sor, when I furst shtepped upon the boords av a doime moosaum in the well-known characther av the Son av the Cannibal King. From that day to this, sor, I have exhibited my charrums to the deloighted eyes av the populus fer tin cints per look. I have been a Zulu Chafetain, a Tattooed Grake, a Noted Malay Pirate, a Bushman from Australier, an' afther a public career which there ben't no better, I am to this day, sor, to this day a Wild Man from Barneo. Widout the natcheral advantages which a ginerous Heaven has besthowed upon you, sor, or upon my honored frind, Misther Kwang, the Chinaze Giant, or upon Maddlemerzelle Bristelli, the bearded Woman, or upon Ko-ko, the T'ree-Headed Girrul,—widout sich natcheral advantages, sor, for to raise me at wanst to the front rank av Frakes, my coorse has been wan av worruk, sor. That worruk has been done; my name as the greatest living Wild Man from Barneo is writ, sor, in letthers av goold upon fame's highest pin—er, pinister! There, sor, it is to-day, and shall I now—"

"Billy," replied the queer little man, "you shall not. Your vords is werry booterful an' werry true. This 'ere bizness of bringin' in Nurse Connellys, an' Marie Wan Zandts, an' the huncles an' hants an' neffies an' nieces an' gran'mothers belonging to influential murderers an' Young Napoleons uv Finance an' sich, is a-puttin' the persitions uv legitermate Freaks in peril. I speaks as the Gran' Worthy Sublime an' Mighty Past High Master uv the Brother'ood an' Sister'ood uv Hanimated Freaks, an' I says hit vont' do! Our rights an' liberties is not thus to be er—is they, Billy?"

"Sor, they air not. They—"

"Vell, then, Billy, you shall come before the Brother'ood an' say so. You shall say it this werry mornin' vith your best langwidge. Vith that tongue o' yours, Billy, an' that 'ere himposin' presence, ef you honly ad' a crook in yer back or ef yer heye vos honly in the middle uv yer 'ed, Billy, you'd be the leadin' Freak on herth!"

"HEXCUSE ME, BILLY," HE SAID, "I NEVER WIOLATE MY PRINCERPLES."

With this genial and deserved tribute, which Mr. O'Fake received most graciously, the dwarf tumbled from his keg, which tumbled also in its turn, raked a heavy overcoat and a rough fur cap from a dark closet, and having got himself into them, he begged Billy to accompany him without delay.

The Brotherhood and Sisterhood of Animated Freaks was and is one of the most important and distinguished of the labor organizations of New York. Its membership is composed, as its name implies, of the ladies and gentlemen actually engaged in the entertainment of the public by the exhibition of their interesting bodies. Its purposes are to encourage social pleasures among its members, and to protect them against the encroachments of domineering managers. Such an organization was made necessary by the continued aggressions of the managerial classes, who were led by their unbridled greed to resort to all kinds of unjust expedients whereby to grind down and trample under foot the poor and needy Freak. This sort of foul injustice went on from year to year, rendering the Freaks more and more dependent on the opulent and tyrannical managers, until the wrongs resultant from it cried to heaven for vengeance. At last, from the depths of their misery the Freaks arose and with one masterful effort they threw off their base shackles and declared themselves free.

It was truly a majestic movement. The Brotherhood was firmly established in all parts of America and Great Britain, and it duly resolved that no one should hereafter be a Freak, or be tolerated in the society of Freaks, who was not a member of the Brotherhood in good standing. It resolved that no manager should employ any one claiming to be a Freak who was not thus rendered legitimate. It resolved to various purports, and in phrases most solemn the majesty of the manhood and womanhood of the freakly profession was vindicated.

The managers, of course, retaliated in kind. They organized a trust. They classified the Freaks and rated them. The relations between labor and capital engaged in the museum industry became thereby greatly strained, but as yet no actual rupture had occurred. All hoped in the public interest to avert such a catastrophe, but each side felt that a fierce struggle was imminent.

Only some such incident as had been supplied in the enterprising stroke of business accomplished by Tony Scollop was needed to fan the sparks of resentment into a flame. The flame was already burning in the bosom of Mr. Billy O'Fake, and when he and the dwarf reached the Brotherhood's headquarters they were ready to perform the functions of a torch.

The Executive Council of the Brotherhood, District No. 6, F. I. M. X. T. S. Z., was about to hold a meeting. The Council was composed of seven eminent Freaks—Sim Boles, the Double-Jointed Wonder; Bony Perkins, the Ossified Man; Duffer Leech, the Man with the Phenomenal Skull; Miss Tilly Boles, the Beautiful Mermaid of the Southern Sea; Mrs. Smock, the Bearded Circassian Beauty; Mr. Billy O'Fake, the Wild Man from Borneo, and the President of the Brotherhood, Runty, the Dwarf. These ladies and gentlemen were the leaders, nay, the fathers and mothers of the organization, distinguished for their sagacity, resolution and prudence.

The arrival of Mr. O'Fake and the Dwarf completed the council, which proceeded promptly to business. Runty took the chair, and in a few earnest and well-chosen words, he dispatched the Ossified Man for a pitcher of beer. The transaction of other routine business occupied the attention of the council for a brief while, but it soon gave way to the pressing business of the hour. This came in the shape of a resolution presented by Mr. O'Fake, in these words:

Whereas, Mr. T. Scollop, manager of the Universal Dime Museum of Natural Wonders, has seen fit to involve our honorable profession in disgrace by the employment for exhibition as an Animated Freak of Grandmother Cruncher, so called; and,

Whereas, The said Grandmother Cruncher is not a member of this Honorable Brotherhood, nor a Freak, but merely a person of vulgar notoriety; and,

Whereas, The said employment by the said T. Scollop of the said Female is in violation of Paragraph 13 of Article 210 of Section 306 of Chapter 194 of Book 8 of the Constitution and By-Laws of this Honorable Brotherhood, therefore be it,

RESOLVED, That a committee of three members of this Council be appointed by the Grand Worthy Sublime and Mighty Past High Master to see the said T. Scollop and to inform him of the displeasure which his course herein set forth has excited in this Council, and to insist upon the immediate discharge of the said Cruncher.

"Wid the Chair's permission," said Mr. O'Fake, when his resolutions had been read, "I will spake a worrud wid regard to the riserlooshuns. Sor, I hav no apolergy to make for thim riserlooshuns. They manes business. We are threatened, sor, wid a didly pur'l. It has not come upon us uv a sudden, sor, not to wanst. It is a repetition, sor, av an ould offince, an' I am here, sor, in this reshpicted prisence, sor, to say that the toime has come fer this Brotherhood to make its power filt!"

Mr. O'Fake brought his clinched fist down upon the back of the Chair in front of him with a smart tap and looked proudly at the admiring faces of his fellow-members. Mr. O'Fake was eminent for his attainments as a speaker, and well he knew it. A murmur of applause broke out as he stopped, but he stilled it with a majestic wave of the hand.

"Sor," he continued, "I am wan av those which belaves that the managers nades a lesson. They nades to be towld, sor, that Frakes is not dogs. They have gone on in their coorse—"

At this point a shrill "Mr. Cheerman!" sounded out from the rear of the hall, and to the great indignation of Mr. O'Fake and to everybody else's surprise, Mr. Duffer Leech, the Man with the Phenomenal Skull, was observed to be standing with his arm lifted and his index finger extended towards the Chair.

Mr. O'Fake was much too astonished at Mr. Leech's audacity to express himself. The Chair looked from one gentleman to the other in perplexity, mysteriously winking at Mr. Leech and nodding at Mr. O'Fake as if to call the attention of the one to the fact that the other was already addressing the council. These repeated gestures having produced no other effect than to draw another "Mr. Cheerman!" from Mr. Leech, the dwarf was moved to inquire, "Vell, Duffer, vot's hup?"

"I wants to know wot's all dis talkin' about. I ain't got all day to sit here and listen to chin-moosic. Wot's de trouble?"

It was easy to see that Duffer had been drinking. No man in his senses would have ventured so rudely to have checked the flow of Mr. O'Fake's oratory. Duffer had clearly been drinking, and the lion whose anger he had roused turned upon him quickly.

"Phwat's the throuble!" he repeated, sarcastically. "I should say the throuble was plain enough. If the gintleman has any difficulty seein' it now, he won't long. It'll take the farm av snakes, sor, an' little rid divils wid long tails in doo toime!"

Mr. O'Fake spoke with much dignity and great effect. In the roar of laughter which followed Duffer perceived he had been vanquished and in some confusion he sat down, while his victor proceeded:

"The offince minshuned in me riserlooshuns is a blow at the daily brid av us all, sor. If any ould woman kin be placed in the froont rank av Frakes fer the rayson that her gran'son killed another ould woman, wull ye tell me, sor, phwat becomes av our janius an' harrud work? Sor, I am bould to say that yersilf, honored as ye are fer hevin' the biggest hid on the shmallest body in the world, had yer hid been as big as a base dhrum an' yer body as shmall as a marble, ye would be regarded as av no impartance in comparison wid this ould witch av a Gran'mother Cruncher."

The impression produced by Mr. O'Fake's remarks was evidently deep and painful. He sat down amid silence which was presently broken by the shrill voice of Duffer.

"Mr. Cheerman," said Duffer. "I rise to a p'int o' order."

"Pint o' vot?" inquired the Chair.

"Order, sir, order!" cried Duffer, who had long been a member of an East Side debating club.

"Vell, I hunderstands you, Duffer, hall as far's you've vent. But it's wery himportant, me boy, vot you horders a pint of. If it's a pint of vhisky, vhy, all right; but if it's honly a pint of beer when there's seven hon'able ladies an' gents—"

"I bigs the Chair's pardon," interrupted Mr. O'Fake, "but the Chair labors under a slight misaper—ahem!" Mr. O'Fake finished the word with a cough. It was a cough which he always kept ready for use in that way whenever needed. "The gintleman manes he objects to the persadin's."

"He does, does 'e? Vell, if that's vot 'e means, 'e hexpresses hisself in a werry poor vay," answered the Chair, directing a look at Duffer which precipitated him at once into his seat.

Mrs. Smock, the Circassian Beauty, said very decidedly that she didn't want any Grandmother Crunchers on the platform with her, and what was the use of having a Brotherhood if you didn't stop such things, which was debasing as everybody knew, and made her blood just boil every time it happened for she couldn't stand having her rights took away and wasn't going to. These energetic remarks decided the Chair to act.

"Vell," he said, "it happears to be a go. The Chair happoints hisself an' Billy an' Sim Boles, an' the sooner ve sees Tony the sooner vill the band begin to play. If you don't think there'll be moosic as'll make your ears 'um, you don't know Tony Scollop."

The Chair thereupon descended from its lofty place, and with characteristic promptness worked itself into its hat and coat. The occasion was felt by all to be somewhat solemn, and murmurs of advice arose to each of the committee as to the best method of proceeding. It was agreed that the other members of the council should remain in the headquarters until the committee's return.

Runty considered himself something of a diplomat, and he let it be understood while on the way to Mr. Scollop's office that he would present the case. They found Mr. Scollop in an amiable humor and most happy to see them. There was a pause after the greetings, and to relieve it Mr. Scollop remarked again that it was a fine day.

"So it is," rejoined Runty, "vich in combination with the natur' of hour business haccounts for hour smilin' faces."

"That's right," said Tony. "Only if I was you I wouldn't smile in the sun. Three such smilin' faces as yours turned right up at him would produce a shadder, Runty. Now, what are you fellows up to? Some Brotherhood game, I'll bet a hat."

"Wot a werry hactive mind!" cried Runty admiringly. "If you vos to guess again you'd hit the game itself an' save us playin' it."

"No, you'd better lead off."

"Vell, then, clubs is trumps, an' we have got a big von vith a knot on the hend for Gran'mother Cruncher—see?"

Mr. Scollop smiled thoughtfully and said he saw. "I see a long ways," he added. "Cruncher is upstairs now, and the public is piling in head over heels to see her. Her portographs is selling like hot cakes and the more you kicks the more she'll be worth to me. Fact is, I wish you would raise a disturbance. There's nothin' like judicious advertisin' in this mooseum business. It would be worth a little something to have a nice, hard strike. Now, then, do you see?"

Runty smiled in his turn and also said he saw. "If that's vot you vant," he said, "you've got it. The strike is on, an' afore you gets through with Gran'mother Cruncher you'll have so much o' the same kind o' notoriety that you an' her'll make a team, an' you both orter grow rich by just hex'ibitin' of your two selves!"

THERE STOOD THE NOBLE OLD LADY IN ALL HER PATHETIC BEAUTY.

"Capital!" cried Mr. Scollop in much excitement, ringing his bell vigorously. "This is the best thing 'ats happened to me in ten years. Hey, there, you, Dick! Rush around the corner an' get a canvas painted—make it big—fifteen by twenty feet, and great big black and red letters. Come now, be quick! Take down the words: 'Strike!' Make each letter two feet long! 'Our Freaks Fight Grandmother Cruncher! They Refuse To Exhibit Along With The Old Lady! Jealous Of Her Dazzling Beauty! Manager Scollop Stands Firm! Says He Will Be Loyal To Grandmother Cruncher Till The Heavens Fall! Not A Freak Left! But Grandmother Cruncher Remains Nobly At Her Post! Thousands Shake Her By The Hand! She Is Now Making A Speech To The Multitude!

Hurry Up To Hear Her Thrilling Words! Come One! Come All! Only Ten Cents!'

"There, got it down?" continued the Manager, breathlessly. "Got it all down? Then rush off, Dick! By the great horn spoon! Was there ever such a stroke of luck as this! Now, Runty, you fellows hurry up to your headquarters, so's to be there when the reporters come. Tell 'em the whole business. Tell 'em you'll never give in! Tell 'em it's a battle to the death! I'll send up a couple o' kegs o' beer and a lot o' cigars. Be lively, now."

Mr. Scollop sprang from his chair and ran upstairs in frantic haste to give directions for rendering the exhibition-room as commodious as possible, leaving Runty and his fellow-committeemen in quite a state of mind.

"Vell!" said the dwarf, drawing a prolonged breath and elevating his eyebrows with a curious expression of mingled surprise and dismay, "'ere's vot I calls a go!"

Bony Perkins rubbed his ossified eyes with his ossified knuckles and observed that it looked as if somebody was going to get fooled.

Mr. O'Fake arose majestically from his chair, and looked grimly at his colleagues. "Gintlemen," he said, "he'll be talkin' in another tone within a wake. Bedad, we'll tache him phwat he don't know. We'll send out an appale fer foonds, an' we'll give him all the fight he wants."

Mr. O'Fake's hopeful tone was needed to brace up the drooping courage of his friends. They immediately returned to the council and briefly reported that their grievances had been ignored, and that the strike was on and would be general. Orders were at once issued and forwarded to every museum in New York directing all Freaks straightway to quit exhibiting and appeals were issued to the public and to all labor associations for financial aid. The headquarters were soon in a state of commotion. Mr. Scollop's kegs of beer had arrived and aided greatly in increasing the ardor of everybody's feelings. The Ossified Man surrounded himself with the Fat Woman, Little Bow-Legs and the Chinese Giant, and lectured them long and earnestly on the rights of labor and the tyranny of class rule. Mr. O'Fake delivered a full score of beautiful orations, and the entire Brotherhood agreed that its power should be exerted to the last extreme.

THE OSSIFIED MAN LECTURED LONG AND EARNESTLY.

Meanwhile Mr. Scollop's museum was the scene of an even greater tumult. The enormous "Strike!" placard had been posted and had produced an immediate effect. Vast crowds of people, wild to see Grandmother Cruncher, besieged the ticket-office and packed the exhibition-room, where, upon the platform, elsewise deserted, stood that noble old lady in all her pathetic beauty. Mr. Scollop, in a condition of rapture scarcely possible of portrayal, stood all the afternoon in his private office opening wine for the gentlemen of the press and giving them the fullest information. He truly said he had nothing to conceal. He had made an honest man's contract and he would stand by it till he dropped in his tracks. He was not the man to desert a poor old woman in her sorrow at the bidding of an irresponsible clique of labor bosses. The Freaks did not want to strike, anyhow. They were nagged on to it by their leaders, who were not genuine Freaks at all, but professional agitators. Aside from his duty to Grandmother Cruncher, he was not going to have his business run by outsiders—not if he knew himself! There would be no abandonment of principle or position on his part, the public might depend on it.

Mr. Scollop professed the deepest sorrow at the annoyance and vexation to which the public was exposed by the unfair conduct of the strikers, but he couldn't help it. It was not his fault. He knew he would have the sympathy of all fair-minded people. He would do his best to satisfy his patrons even under these trying circumstances. The museum was open now, as the reporters could easily see, and would be kept open. Grandmother Cruncher would exhibit and would be the great and permanent feature of his show hereafter, Brotherhood or no Brotherhood!

These remarks, amplified and extended, appeared in the papers, together with interviews with the strikers and many thrilling incidents of the struggle. Public interest was aroused in the most general and intense degree, and Mr. Scollop's cashier made daily trips to the bank with a bushel-basket full of dimes. How long the contest would have continued and what the final result would have been are problems too deep for me. But at the end of the first week Grandmother Cruncher's rheumatism was too much for her and she was compelled to retire. Short as was her professional career, it gave her undying fame. In labor circles many ugly rumors are floating about concerning the management of the strike. It is broadly intimated that the whole thing was a "sell," and significant remark is made upon the fact that Runty, the Dwarf, shortly after the strike was ordered off, appeared upon the street scintillating under a new diamond pin. One of the leading daily journals editorially explained the matter by stating that the rheumatism story was a ruse, that public interest in Grandmother Cruncher began to wane, and that thereupon Manager Scollop "fixed the matter up" with the strikers. Tony, however, declares that the Brotherhood gave in, while Runty says it is stronger than ever and more than ever determined to protect the rights of its members. Where the exact truth lies it is far from me to say, but it may be pertinent to mention that Runty and Mr. O'Fake have started a saloon in the Bowery.

THE END.

Milton Keynes UK
Ingram Content Group UK Ltd.
UKHW011142220424
441551UK00007B/765